PENGUIN BOOKS

GIRL ALONE

Rupa Gulab suffers Delhi. This is her first book.

girl alone

rupa gulab

PENGUIN BOOKS

PENGUIN BOOKS
Published by the Penguin Group
Penguin Books India Pvt. Ltd, 11 Community Centre, Panchsheel Park,
New Delhi 110 017, India
Penguin Group (USA) Inc., 375 Hudson Street, New York, NY 10014,
USA
Penguin Group (Canada), 10 Alcorn Avenue, Toronto, Ontario, Canada
M4V 3B2 (a division of Pearson Penguin Canada Inc.)
Penguin Books Ltd, 80 Strand, London WC2R 0RL, England
Penguin Ireland, 25 St Stephen's Green, Dublin 2, Ireland (a division of
Penguin Books Ltd)
Penguin Group (Australia), 250 Camberwell Road, Camberwell, Victoria
3124, Australia (a division of Pearson Australia Group Pty Ltd)
Penguin Group (NZ), cnr Airborne and Rosedale Roads, Albany,
Auckland 1310, New Zealand (a division of Pearson New Zealand Ltd)
Penguin Group (South Africa) (Pty) Ltd, 24 Sturdee Avenue, Rosebank,
Johannesburg 2196, South Africa

Penguin Books Ltd, Registered Offices: 80 Strand, London WC2R 0RL,
England

First published by Penguin Books India 2005

Copyright © Rupa Gulab 2005
Girl Alone is loosely based on Rupa Gulab's column 'Dating Diary' for
Cosmopolitan (India)

Typeset in Perpetua by InoSoft Systems, Noida
Printed at Baba Barkhanath Printers, New Delhi

For Salil:
With Love

acknowledgements

A big hug to all the people who made *Girl Alone* possible.

Madhu Jain and Vishal Dhar at fridaycorporation.com. They commissioned the writing of *Girl Alone*, a diary to be serialized online. Sadly, their lifestyle section shut down before the story could take off;

Priya Ramani, the then editor of *Cosmopolitan* (India), for picking it up and running it in the same format with a new title, 'Dating Diary';

Payal Kohli, who succeeded Priya as the editor of *Cosmopolitan*. She urged me to continue the story for one more year;

My friend Mira Krishnan, who said, 'Hello, why don't you get it published as a book now?';

Old Monk for inspiring me to rewrite my columns as a novel. It was hell, for I had to start from scratch;

Shobhaa Dé for appreciating my manuscript and forwarding it to Penguin;

V.K. Karthika at Penguin for finally, finally, finally putting me where I've always longed to be: on the shelf;

Mum and Dad for giving me their writing talent, their sense of humour and enough rope to hang myself with;

My sisters Roma Circar and Gia Goyal for making encouraging noises with every chapter they read;

My husband Salil Sadanandan and my sister Bunny Gulab for reading every single draft I wrote even though they made it painfully clear that they would have preferred root canals;

My best friend, philosopher and guide, Ranjona Banerji, for enthusiastically throwing herself into my project. She was very, very generous with her time and tips;

My ex art partner and good friend, Hanna Wistrand, for informing me in no uncertain terms that she would design the cover, or else! Lots of emails flew between New Delhi and Stockholm to make it happen;

All my other friends who read a few chapters of the work in progress and were not terribly polite at all. Especially Sonali Ghosh Sen.

It's no good trying to get rid of your own aloneness. You've got to stick to it all your life. Only at times, at times, the gap will be filled in. At times! But you have to wait for the times.

—D.H. Lawrence, *Lady Chatterley's Lover*

one

My mother made me do it. To her goes the credit for my relationship with Low Life, the cretin who emotionally slaughtered me. Admittedly, my hormones had a role to play in it too. They're pretty frisky and not remotely discerning. I mean, they're capable of making me fall in lust with Jack the Ripper. I'm really grateful he's not alive.

Mum made me do a lot of other things too, like giving up my plans for an MA degree. She just wouldn't hear of it. I was silenced with an autocratic, 'Over my dead bod.' Mum used that phrase a lot. She was positively addicted to it, possibly because it sounded powerfully emphatic. She's a fairly pushy person. If I didn't know better, I'd say she was Lady Macbeth in her past life. Don't get me wrong, I love my mother—hey, I would kill for her—but I'm not into blind, unconditional devotion. I hate the way she always tries to run my life and make me live her stupid dreams. Also, I'm perverse.

'All you'll be fit for after an MA is ministering to the needs of ingrates. Get a job, Arti. Get a life,' Mum pleaded.

You know you're a total loser when your mum tells you to get a life. Most Indian mums make you do just the opposite. But then, my mum was brought up differently. Her dad was posted in East Africa when she was a child, and the family joined him there from Pakistan during Partition. Thereafter, they moved to London. 'Not Southall,' Mum would say with a haughty sniff. She took great pains to tell everybody she lived in a very upmarket part of the city, lest they thought her family swept and swabbed Heathrow airport like other sad Indian immigrants. That's perhaps why she never pronounced 'isn't it' as 'innit' or addressed people as 'love' and 'duckie' or said stuff like 'You're a right caution, you are', thank god. The colourful Eliza Doolittle's 'gorblimey' too wasn't part of her vocabulary; 'ruddy' was more like it. She came to India to get married to a good Hindu boy and finally settled down in Calcutta without suffering a major culture shock. That's because although the British Raj was officially over, its influence still lingered. Bengali brown sahibs spoke the Queen's English way better than the Queen herself. Christmas was still *burra din* and celebrated with almost as much fervour as Durga Puja. Park Street's shop windows were decked with sprigs of holly, tinsel streamers and tacky scenes from the Nativity. Calcutta had a rich nightclub legacy too, with places like The Golden Slipper, where people did the jive and tango to stuff like *Hey Mambo*, *House with the bamboo door, Yellow polka dot bikini* and *Stupid Cupid*.

Anyway, to get back to Mum. What she, in her muddled, well-meaning way wanted me to do, was to really enjoy my freedom before I settled down, something that she wasn't allowed to do, and she just couldn't understand why I was getting antsy about it. But I was an inhibited, insecure coward. I hated new experiences with a passion. Honestly, I preferred comfort to excitement, I still do. I tried to reason with Mum about the MA course. In vain.

'Oh come on, Ma! I can always teach after getting my degree,' I protested. I had these visions of myself as a great academic with radical takes on literature— the sort who'd inspire undergrads to slash their wrists if they weren't assigned tutorials with me. My burning ambition was to introduce rock as an integral part of modern English literature. I seriously believe that some rock lyricists are New Age poets, even more talented than Ted Hughes or Maya Angelou. And my second ambition was to get Indian wannabe rock bands to stop doing lousy covers and prove their mettle by composing music for some of the greatest poems in the world like T.S. Eliot's *The Love Song of J. Alfred Prufrock*. I was positive that words like 'Like a patient etherised upon a table', could be set to edgy, mind-blowing music—the sort that goes down well with a joint.

Mum played her winning card then. I don't know how she manages it, but she always has an indefatigable supply of aces tucked up her sleeve. 'Teaching isn't going to make you financially independent. But if that's what you really want to do, more's the pity. We'd better find a husband to support you in that case.'

That's how Mum won, even though Dad was on my side. I didn't want to get married just then. And particularly not to a loser who put an ad in the papers. People like that are usually personality-challenged. I wanted to find someone on my own but I really didn't know where to look. None of the men I'd dated so far had even inspired me to take off my 'To Let' sign, leave alone my clothes.

There aren't too many jobs going when you're just an English literature graduate. Perhaps that's why we had very few guys in our class. Journalism and advertising were really the only two options available then, which is why I'd applied for both. Journalism was my first choice; it seemed the more intellectual thing to do. With my fucked luck, an advertising agency responded to my CV first. That's how I got a job as a trainee copywriter in Bombay. Mum was over the moon. She was certain Bombay would make me less tight-assed (though she used a more politically correct word for it). I wasn't sure I wanted the job at all. It seemed kind of frivolous to me, writing trashy, mindless jingles for the hoi polloi instead of literary critiques. She damn well made sure I took it though, by intently circling sections of the matrimonial columns in my presence—in blood-red ink. She's *that* brutal. That woman can do anything if she puts her mind to it: move mountains, shame Bill Clinton into turning celibate, even, perhaps, make bin Laden convert to Christianity. The CIA could really use her.

My fate was signed and sealed. Accommodation in a working women's hostel was organized by one of her friends. All that remained to be done was for me to be delivered. Mum found someone to do that too. Someone who knew someone who knew someone who knew someone whose nephew was visiting from Bombay. That's the way people in Calcutta get things done; everyone's part of one big, happy, helpful (and horribly nosy) family. He was leaving the same day as I was and his role was to escort me to the hostel, since I didn't know my way around the city. That's when I first met Low Life.

We were introduced to each other at the airport and I detested him on sight. Mum thought he was suave and I didn't have to be a mind-reader to know what she was thinking: Arti gets a job and, hello, a husband working for a—hold your breath—Fortune 500 company too. She could have dined on that for centuries. I just found him offensively smarmy. I can't deny that he was dishy in a run-of-the-mill North Indian sort of way (tall, fair, sort of aristocratic nose—the usual), but he was annoyingly affected and exuded an I'm-so-happening air. I wasn't happening back then. Things didn't even happen around me. I could even make Swiss clocks stop.

I hated him first off when he asked me to call him Sandy, even though his name was Sandip. Like I was some foreigner who couldn't pronounce Indian names easily, or someone he'd played peek-a-boo with in his infancy. I didn't trust easy familiarity in those days. I used to think distance spoke breeding. What really put me off was that he wasn't even looking at me when the introductions were made. He was busy checking out a hot babe sashaying past in a tee that was at least six sizes too small. Hey, even Dad was looking, but not in a hungry, lip-smacking sort of way, if you know what I mean.

It didn't end there. On the flight, Low Life made me want to reach for the airsickness bag more than once. I was reading this book, *Madame Bovary*, and was really into it. He had some trashy *Sharky's Machine* kind of best-seller that evidently wasn't gripping enough, because he kept interrupting me with inane conversation, the sort that even airheads would find vapid. I was just about ready to break his smarmy face when he tipped my hand over to check out the cover of my book. He let out this low whistle and looked impressed. 'Wow! You must be really deep.'

And you must be beyond-belief shallow, I thought. I mean, I'm contemptuous of people who think that a book by a French author has to be erudite. After all, they have porn and hack writers in France too. 'Actually, it's just sleazy stuff about a woman who's cheating on her husband.' I had to put Flaubert down to shut him up. I was *that* desperate. I'd have committed third-degree homicide too, if that's what it took.

'Really?' His eyes flickered with excitement. He practically snatched the book out of my hand and hungrily flipped through it. He looked disappointed and handed it back. I think he was expecting the smutty, Harold Robbins genre of sleaze. 'The words are really big, huh? Do you carry a dictionary around or do you just ignore them?'

'I *know* the meanings. I don't know about you, but I went to school *and* college.'

I could swear he mouthed the word 'bitch'. We ignored each other and were silent for a while till I got this overpowering whiff of alcohol. He was desperately hitting his hip flask like a camel at an oasis. That made me paranoid because everyone thought he was with me, and back then I used to be a stickler for rules—hey, convent education disciplines people better than the army. 'You see that sign there? It says consumption of alcohol is not permitted on domestic flights,' I pointed out in a prissy, class-monitor way.

'Is that so? We've already established that I can't read, and I don't know you well enough to believe you,' he shot back, looking pissed off.

I gave up. The next and last word we said to each other was at the hostel. It was 'goodbye'. If anyone had told me then that he would become my grand passion, I'd have made her rinse out her mouth. With toilet disinfectant.

Anyway, I forgot about him the minute the cab drove away and took in my new home away from home. I'd imagined the hostel to be a depressing, *Oliver Twist* kind of place and was pleasantly surprised. It was light and airy and had a nice sort of buzz. The warden, an ageing Goan spinster, seemed sort of decent too (then) but a bit batty. She had this caged parrot on her desk and was teaching it to say 'I love you'. Monica and Jyotsna (Mo and Jo), the two people she'd asked to escort me to my room, held her in utter contempt. Jo witheringly dismissed her as a desperado and Monica, the sensible one (after all, she's in finance), told her that Twisted Spinster Warden was only doing the practical thing here: there was a ten-to-one chance that the parrot would say those three little words to her before a man did.

Mo and Jo. Mojo. A powerfully sexy word, popularized by two of my favourite people: Jim Morrison and Austin Powers. I secretly wondered if Monica and

Jo had ever made the connect, but I didn't point it out—
hey, I'd just met them. I kind of warmed to them instantly
though. They were amusing and cool, just the sort of
people I enjoy hanging out with. The only thing about
them that struck me as a bit odd was that they were
more than friends. They had this tension between them,
you know, the kind siblings share, where you bicker
madly like you totally can't stand each other. Maybe it
was because they'd been chums at the hostel for so long.

The moment we entered the room, I almost keeled
over. There was this stench of—how do I describe it?—
six-month-old dead fish in a used sports sock. Jo saw
my nose twitch and grinned. 'Oh, you'll get used to that.
It's only Bombay Duck.'

'God, I didn't know ducks stank,' I wheezed. It's
really difficult to talk when you're trying hard not to
breathe.

Monica and Jo rolled on the floor with mirth. It
turned out that Bombay Duck was a fish. I always knew
Calcutta University was superior to Bombay University.
I mean, these Bombayites couldn't even tell the difference
between scales and feathers. I sprayed the room with my
prized bottle of Estée Lauder and collapsed on the bed.
The last words I remember saying to them were, 'Any
idea where I can get a gas mask from?'

Monica and Jo turned out to be my guardian angels
and the best friends I ever had. Oh, I'd had decent

friends in Calcutta; while I wasn't an extrovert, I wasn't exactly the shy, retiring type either. But we never poured our hearts out to each other, just did things together and discussed books, music, guys, ambitions and stuff. Communal living makes people more open and confiding and being in the hostel was like being on touchy-feely Oprah: dirty linen was always being washed in public and nobody shied away from discussing deep, dark secrets about incestuous relationships and eating disorders and things.

Monica's murky secret was that she'd been having an affair with a married man for years. Jo's was that she had once posed nude for an ex and he *still* had the negatives. Mine was that I had smoked a joint with friends in college and loved it, but didn't have the courage to try it again—I was *that* depressing! Also, I was scared of being caught out. I knew Mum religiously read all those leaflets they hand out on street corners, you know, the ones that go, 'Is your kid doing drugs? Look for these signs'. Mum was always keenly searching me for clues of waywardness. I think she privately hoped that I had some redeeming character flaw or something. She'd always accused me of being too good to be true. Honestly, in those days the only flaw I had was attitude. Big-time attitude. But nothing else really. Apart from being a closet cough-syrup addict. But hey, it was medicine and medicine's good for you!

Jo and Monica eased me into the city and in less than six months I knew all the vitally important things there are to know about a new place: quaint book and music shops, where to get fake doctor's certificates from if you wanted to do a bunk, areas to avoid in case of communal riots, restaurants that serve food that remind you of home and suchlike. They'd also introduced me to the joys of alcohol. I'd never had anything more potent than a shandy before, and I took to it like a Bombay Duck to water. I had them to thank for my new image— not just the way I looked, but my mental make-up too. They'd skilfully stripped me of most of my tight-assed inhibitions over time. There was so much to experience, so many things to try, I felt like a butterfly emerging from a chrysalis or something. Forget recognizing myself in the mirror, I didn't even recognize my soul any more. I'd changed *that* much and, frankly, I liked what I'd become. I was almost happening in fact. I just hadn't gone all the way yet. My 'To Let' sign was still flashing.

Over time, I grew to love Bombay so much that I'd even decided I wanted to die there and have my ashes scattered over my favourite haunts: Toto's Garage, my favourite grungy pub where they play rock and only rock, soppy shit be damned; The Sea Lounge, for lingering cups of hot chocolate and a fabulous view of the Gateway of India; Gajalee, for divine oysters, clams, crabs and other Malvani seafood specialities; Samovar, the cafe at Jehangir Art Gallery, where chilled-out beery afternoons stretch into languid evenings with lazy discussions on life, the universe and everything; Rang Bhawan, the rock-show joint, where big international bands sometimes perform and decent Indian bands do derivative originals and covers that are bearable only if you have loads of wax jammed in your ears; and, of course, Marine Drive, with its glittering, glamorous arc of lights appropriately called the Queen's Necklace. You know, you haven't lived if you've never walked down this promenade during the monsoon. Sometimes, gigantic waves leap out of the swollen Arabian Sea and drench you completely. It's absolutely exhilarating, a completely mood-altering experience. The way I see it, Bombay's the Big Mango, India's equivalent of the Big Apple, where art and commerce live cheek by jowl in an open, cosmopolitan atmosphere. You know that song, Art Garfunkel's *Heart in New York*, the lyrics remind me of Bombay, a city throbbing with vitality and people with heart, despite the fact that they also have money on their minds. I revelled in the freedom and anonymity the city gave me and even became immune to the stench of Bombay Duck.

What stank more than that was Low Life. Unfortunately, I bumped into the cretin a few years later. I was at this new, wannabe swank pub in Colaba with Jo and Monica, and we were drinking ourselves silly, taking full advantage of their 'Buy one, get one free' promo. Monica had started this animated conversation about why eight out of ten women dislike caramel custard and blow jobs with equal passion. I think the conclusion we'd arrived at was that it was a consistency issue—they're both slimy. Jo suddenly nudged me and whispered that this gorgeous hunk was giving me the once-over. I looked up and found myself staring into Low Life's eyes. I recognized the creep immediately and leapt up to renew our acquaintance. After all, he *had* done me a favour once. And I was full of bonhomie anyway—alcohol momentarily evicts the nun trapped in my body.

'Hi!'

'Hi! I'm Sandy.' This was said with a wolfish grin. I could swear he was drooling too. He obviously hadn't recognized me. I mean, the smarmy shit thought I was trying to pick him up.

'I know,' I said dryly. 'I'm Arti. From Cal. The person who travelled with you to Bombay, what, three years ago?'

His jaw dropped. 'You look different.'

'Well, thanks.' I took that as a compliment. That's because I knew I looked terrible in Cal. Frumpy and grungy. I mean, I used to pinch Dad's shirts because they were loose. My dress sense made me look like I'd walked out of the pages of fashion magazines called *Vague* or *Hell* as opposed to chic glossies like *Vogue* or *Elle*.

'No, really,' he continued, still drooling. 'If you'd looked like this then, you'd probably be the mother of my babies by now.'

'Hey, you still get your pickup lines from Harold Robbins?'

'Yeah, he gets better results than your French porn writers, you know.'

I had to laugh at that and the ice was broken. I was about to get back to my table, but Low Life insisted I have a drink with him. Oh, he could be devastatingly charming when he felt like it. He was like that girl in the nursery rhyme (I forget the name) that went, 'When she was good she was very, very good, and when she was bad she was horrid.' I accepted. We got into this discussion about books. He confessed that he'd never read P.G. Wodehouse before, because it was only available in Penguin, and he'd always assumed that books with a Penguin logo were terminally boring classic types like *Twenty Thousand Leagues under the Sea* or something. I found him disarming. All the guys I used to hang out with in Calcutta were cheap pseudo-intellectuals who'd go all out to persuade you that they were better read than you were. Hey, they'd even quote from *Beowulf* or *The Rise and Fall of the Roman Empire* during a date, hoping to impress the knickers off you! And then, I felt overcome by this comic book KABOOM effect and my hormones started exploding like firecrackers. It was the most amazing chemistry I'd ever experienced. Within a few weeks I'd graduated to my first lesson in advanced biology. I became a total whiz at practicals—hell, I could give rabbits serious competition. And four years later, Low Life taught me another lesson, one I'll never forget: men suck.

two

The best-laid plans of mice and men may go awry, but Mum's plans never do. Well, usually never. This was the one time in my life when I realized that she was fallible, hell, even mortal. Low Life was her favourite son-in-law and we weren't even married. As far as she was concerned, she'd shown great leniency and Western open-mindedness in allowing us to have a four-year courtship, it was about time the screws were tightened. I have to admit that I had been getting antsy about it too. I didn't fancy the idea of wearing gold-plated dentures on my wedding day, but my Barkis didn't appear to be willin'. Despite the fact that I knew more about him than anybody else in the world did, including his precious mother. I knew that he'd made out with a guy once, just to check it out. I knew that he loved fried eggs with a runny yolk. I knew that he had to sleep with his right toe sticking out from under the sheet for some inexplicable reason. I knew that the moles on his back formed the shape of Orion. I knew that arty types made him feel insecure which is why he always bad-mouthed them. I knew his pet nightmare: taking a driving test with a female examiner and failing miserably. Hey, I'd even tweezed the stray, unwieldy hairs growing on his ears! That's the kind of intimacy strong marriages are built on. With Mum egging me on, I started voicing my where-do-we-go-from-here anxiety.

I got my cue after I'd got back from a two-day shoot. I'd gone over to his place and was enveloped in a big bear hug. 'Hey Arti, I missed you.'

'Don't Miss me, Mrs me instead, goddammit.' Bad pun, but it got my point across. The only hitch was that typically, I'd chosen the worst time imaginable to bring up the M-word. A cricket match was blaring on TV. 'I'm serious, Sandy. Do you love me?'

'Huh? I loved that *Cosmo* turn-on thing you did to me last Saturday.'

'I know you lust me, Sandy. I'm talking about love, you know, till-death-do-us-part stuff. You savvy?'

The sod wasn't even listening to me; he was deeply engrossed in the match. 'Not now, Arti. Man, Tendulkar's on a roll. Six!'

I had to do it then, something Dad had warned me never ever to do to a man. I was prepared to face the consequences: I switched off the TV, mid-match.

'Whaddyadothatfor? Are you crazy? Gimme the remote!' Low Life panicked like I'd unplugged his life-support system or something.

'Answer my question first. Will we ever get married?'

'I never said we wouldn't,' he said, hedging as always.

'You never said we would, either.' I was determined to resolve the issue—once and for all.

'Dammit, there's an India–Pakistan match going on. That's more important than bloody marriage!'

He wrestled the remote away from me and the TV beamed on. I courted danger again: I stood in front of the screen, blocking his view. 'So will we or won't we?'

'Just give me some time.'

'Then give me a time frame, dammit. When? When you become a bloody CEO? When your pension cheques are in the mail? Tell me when, Sandy, when? Because I don't want to have wrinkles on my wedding day. They won't go with my outfit!' I was so livid, I was screaming like a fisherwoman with a bad case of PMS.

'We'll talk about it after the match. Deal?'

'You bet we will! And the sooner, the better. This whole bloody marriage thing is turning me into a catamaran.'

'It's turning you into a boat?' Low Life looked puzzled. That was something I found most endearing about him. Every time I used a big word, he'd get these deep, ploughmark-like furrows on his brows. He was good with numbers, though. Quite a whiz, in fact.

'God no, dumb ass! A catamaran also means a

cantankerous woman,' I enlightened him.

'What's "cantankerous" mean?'

I flung a cushion at him in reply.

'I give up! I'll marry you, Arti,' he conceded with a grin.

'You will? Before my twenty-eighth birthday?'

'Before your twenty-ninth birthday.'

'Really?'

'Yeah, I kind of like the idea of owning a walkie-talkie dictionary.'

We fell into each other's arms. And you know what? He was looking deep into my eyes for a change, not at the TV screen.

Big words really turned him on. But evidently cheap floozies turned him on even more. As I was to discover a few months later, on my twenty-eighth birthday, the day I officially became the target consumer for anti-wrinkle and anti-cellulite potion ads. Funny, but I was feeling gloomy enough before the party, poring over an ad for anti-cellulite gel, when Monica popped into my room to say bye. She couldn't make it to my bash on account of an unavoidable official dinner with the worldwide CEO of Saloman Brothers or someplace equally jaw-dropping. She was fast-track material.

'Why the long face? It's your birthday. Smile, goddamit!'

'Can't. It'll deepen the laugh lines around my eyes.

Hey, check out this ad. It's making me hyperventilate.'

Monica glanced at it coolly, then tossed it aside, preening in front of my mirror. She was wearing a heavy *kanjeevaram* sari and looked really sophisticated. 'So maybe I have better skin. I'm thirty-one and the lines don't show yet.'

I had to get back at her for that. 'Not in dim lighting at any rate. Hey these are ten-watt bulbs, remember? And if you don't get that promotion, we'll know you didn't put out tonight,' I added bitchily.

Jo entered, dressed in these really tacky-wacky yet chic clothes (she used to get a whopping discount from practically every on-the-make designer in Bombay because she was a lifestyle journo) and added her bit to that. 'She's right, Monica. Ten out of ten women who don't put out don't get promoted.'

'Ha, ha, bitches,' Monica said icily, and swept out with a regal air.

Low Life was throwing the party at his swank Altamount Road company apartment. Most of the people there were his stuffy, starchy marketing pals. I'd just invited a few people from work I really liked, like my art partner, Tenaz, and a handful of others. And Jo was there, of course, with Lust Bug, her new male acquisition, thank god, or else I'd have died of mortification or a coronary—whichever came first. I was getting almost dizzy playing hostess, circulating clockwise and anticlockwise, when I passed by the bedroom door and heard this frenzied moaning. Jo and I exchanged mock-lewd glances. We were cracking up, till I heard this horribly familiar voice saying, 'Where the hell does this unhook from? Front or back?'

Jo didn't succeed in holding me back. Nothing, not even an earth mover can, when I get going. I'm made of sterner stuff. Hey, sometimes Mum's genes do show up! I shot into the room to find Low Life in, of all places, his walk-in closet. He was getting steamy with a woman who had the unmistakable air of a creature to the kennel born. And he was doing things to her that would make even Hugh Hefner blush. Hell, it made me see red too. Bimbo Dogess looked embarrassed at being caught out and scuttled away like a cockroach in search of a dark corner—the usual case of natural homing instincts coming to the fore. Low Life, however, was unremorseful. He shrugged in a cool, fuck-you way and gave me the classic male line, the one that no woman can argue with. Well, not successfully, at any rate. 'Look, I'm sorry, but, like, I need space, okay? And you were freaking me out with that marriage shit.'

'In which case, you made the right choice,' I began. Typically, I dissolved into tears mid-sentence. What I'd wanted to tell him was that he'd made the right choice in his space quest, because Bimbo Dogess had a lot of

it between her ears. Wide enough to fit the Empire State
Building horizontally. It really was too bad that I couldn't
get it in. That's one of the most annoying things that
happen to me. My best one-liners are rarely aired in
public. They just lurk around in my head so only I know
how sharp I am. Jo, keeper of my sanity, thrust a tissue
into my hand. I honked unbecomingly into it as an
interested crowd gathered. Face it, *everyone* loves sleaze.
And I decided to give it to them. Hey, when it rains, it
pours! As Jo and Lust Bug attempted to bundle me out
of the flat, I heard someone ask, 'Were they having
problems or something?'

    And I shouted out, 'Yes! With his libido.' I also told
all the men at large that if Bimbo Dogess refused to give
them her number, to look it up on a public loo wall. I
was *that* angry.

    Once in the cab, all three of us were silent. Lust
Bug squirmed. Like most men, he hated scenes. Jo
kept darting anxious looks at me like I was going to
leap out mid-drive and fling myself under the wheels
of a double-decker or something. That made me feel
even more paranoid and I launched into my usual 'Why
me?' tirade when she tentatively asked how I was feeling.
I do that a lot. Mum swears that 'Why me' were the
first two words I spoke as a baby, despite the fact that
she'd been coaxing me to say 'Ma'. She's always
maintained that my persecution mania could give even

Hasidic Jews a serious complex. She's lying through her teeth, of course, but I secretly have to admit that she's right about one thing: those two little words have been on the tip of my tongue for most of my life. That night was the one time I really meant it though. With all my heart, liver, kidneys, lungs—hell, my whole anatomy!

'Why is it only me who has to find out this way? Any normal person would have discovered her boyfriend's infidelity in a more discreet place—like a laundry room, for fuck's sake,' I whined.

'Why laundry room? Oh, okay, you mean lipstick-on-the-collar evidence.' Jo catches on fairly fast. One of the things I really enjoy about her is that she's always on the ball.

'Exactly. So why did I have to discover him with fresh lipstick on his lips in front of about a million people? Do I have this desperately bad karma or something?'

'It's not such a big deal. They're friends,' Jo feebly attempted to placate me. Like I hadn't noticed that people were getting on their yuppie mobile phones and spreading the word with the fervour of evangelists even before my back was turned. With friends like those, who needed Pakistanis? Well, that's what I thought in those days. These days, India and Pakistan seem to be making an effort to be neighbourly with can-I-borrow-a-cup-of-sugar conversations happening across the border, thank god. I feel really uncomfortable thinking of Shaheen and other deadly nuclear missiles and warheads pointing at me.

So that's how I wound up in my room at 10 p.m. on a Saturday night, just when the city was getting ready to kick up its heels and alcohol and condom sales were going through the roof. There I was, staring at four damp walls, licking my wounds and knocking back the remnants of a bottle of cough syrup. Not because I had a sore throat, but because I needed to regain my equilibrium. I'd discovered its calming, soporific effect when I was about three years old or something, and with a domineering mum like mine, you can't really blame me for getting heavily addicted to it. All through my childhood, I used to spend most of my pocket money on it. Even today, it's the one thing I never leave home without, American Express cards be damned. It always makes me feel comfortably numb when I'm desperately down. Jo was there with me too, playing Ministering Angel. She glanced at the label on the bottle and squawked: 'Hell, this thing contains chloroform, dammit! That's what they knock out frogs with.' I cried even louder at that and she attempted to console me by talking in clichés. 'Ah, forget him, there are lots of good fish in the sea.'

'Give me a break, Jo! I'm not looking for a whale of a time with a sardine or a shark. All I want is the one that got away.' That was the honest truth. I only wanted Low Life then. Nobody else would do. Not even Keanu Reeves and he's unbelievably hot. That's what was so frightening.

Monica joined us when she returned from her hotshot corporate dinner. She hadn't expected me back that night and was curious to see my room lights on. Then she looked at me and cottoned on. Not that it was difficult to figure out that I was going through acute emotional trauma. My eyes were bloodshot and my mascara had streaked. I probably looked like something even a starving Ethiopian lion wouldn't eat.

'Will someone please tell me what's going on?'

'I caught Randy Sandy making out with the first slut handy,' I volunteered, shrugging in a fuck-it way.

Monica's eyes widened. Jo gave her the sordid details in a stage whisper while I was dying inside. It was bad enough seeing it. Hearing about it made it about a million times worse. What I mean is, I was referred to in the third person. That's gossip. And there was going to be a lot of it in the coming days, I'd figured; the grapevine had already started buzzing.

Monica took over in her no-nonsense, practical way, as usual. It's strange, but Jo's really my best friend. When I feel like the lowest life form on earth, she cheers me up. She's the only legal mind-altering substance I know till date. But Monica sorts me out.

I may not enjoy her dry, clinical methods, but they set me straight all right. She categorically informed me that she'd always hated Low Life with a passion. Jo seconded it. As if I hadn't known that already. I also knew that he reciprocated their feelings with equal ardour. Things like this don't really bother me. I don't subscribe to the love me, love my dog philosophy. That's for losers. I would rather subscribe to *Mad* magazine instead and live and let live. Right then, however, I just wanted to be alone. More so because Jo and Monica got into a heated argument and I had enough problems of my own already. It started fairly innocuously, when Monica lit a cigarette and Jo (a rabid, born-again non-smoker) told her it was about time she quit.

'No way. It's easier to give up men than cigarettes,' Monica said firmly.

'So what's stopping you from giving Dev up, then, huh? Get real, Monica. He's never going to leave his wife.'

Monica eyed her archly. Jo was stupid to encroach on personal territory, but I guess she was stressed out with the evening's happenings too, and just wanted to vent.

'True. But I don't want to get married, see? I'm happy with the way things are.'

'Go ahead. Fool yourself.'

Monica got really annoyed. 'Look, he doesn't sleep

with her, dammit! That's all that matters to me, okay? Case closed.'

Jo looked like she was about to make a cutting remark, when I deftly stepped in with a heartbreaking sob. That shut her up instantly. I threw them both out. Jo insisted on bringing her mattress into my room to watch over me, but I refused to let her. 'Hey, chill. I'm not going to deliberately mistake a can of cockroach spray for breath freshener or something. Promise. I just need to sort myself out. Alone.'

Monica shot me a keen look and dragged her out with a dry, 'She'll survive, Jo. We all do.'

I wasn't lying about not intending to snuff out my life. After all, I'd only dated Low Life for about four years. I knew my parents for longer and there was no way, absolutely no way I was going to hurt them over a piece of shit. I can be very reasonable at times. So reasonable, that I even surprise myself into believing that I'm a left-brain kind of person. What I didn't tell them was that I'm a physical coward. Even if I'm driven to slash my wrists, I'd be praying like hell that the blade was blunt. I'm an ace mental survivor, however. I know how to heal myself. All I need is solitude and deep, dark music to see me through.

I have a pretty decent music-to-get-over-cretins collection. Most literature graduates do. After you live and breathe Eliot, Poe and Browning, you can't stomach break-up songs by Michael Bolton and suchlike weedy wimps. They sound like trite nursery rhymes for retards. What I liked best about Browning was *Porphyria's Lover*. I understood why the guy strangled her the instant their passion peaked. I mean, he knew it could never touch such an unbelievably euphoric high again. I only wish Porphyria had been the one to realize that first and kill him instead. That's the problem with women. They're passive in relationships.

I chose Pink Floyd to get me into recovery mode. Hey, grim lyrics like 'Day after day, love turns grey' may sound like pretentious shit on paper, but they help more than Sigmund-fucking-Freud (what good can he do, he's dead; and besides, he'd probably tell me I was miserable because I couldn't have sex with my father or some half-assed crap). I tried to come to terms with the fact that the guy I used to think was a real brick turned out to be just another prick. Just like all the men in this country. Indian men really suck. Out here, a woman doesn't have to do much to be labelled a floozie. You just have to:

1. Drink in a public place: a sure sign that you're loving and, indeed, exceptionally giving—blow jobs included.

2. Smoke on the road: if you do that and not a single man over the age of puberty surreptitiously whispers 'How much?' in your ear, you feel inadequate, like you're having a really awful bad-

hair day.

3. Live in a hostel: that's because the correct spelling of a hostel for women, according to most Indian men, is W-H-O-R-E-S-T-E-L.

And, if you fulfil any of the above sleazy conditions, congratulations! You're taken home to mother—when mother isn't home, of course. They're all full of shit.

three

Time is supposed to heal all wounds. But it moves so slowly, you practically die before the scabs even make an appearance. I didn't feel even 0.00001 per cent better the next day. I felt a lot worse, in fact. Things always look terrible to me in daylight. Night shields me from reality, because it's dark and sort of mysterious and I think maybe this is just a bad dream or something. But during the day, it's different. You know it's over, with this smack-you-in-the-face clarity.

By the time I'd crawled out of bed, everyone in the hostel was aware that I'd been dumped. They looked at me curiously, like I was a brattish Bollywood star who'd run over a pavement dweller in his Pajero or something the night before. Some of the looks were of abject pity, some curious, but mostly they were the smug, she's-finally-got-her-comeuppance kind. Lots of people think I'm a supercilious bitch. And honestly, I had the right to be supercilious among that loser hostel lot. If you met them, you'd agree. Especially if you were from Calcutta. Most people from Calcutta feel superior. We don't just have some of the best academics in the country. We can also boast of the most passionate cricket and football fans, the most authentic Chinese food this side of the Great Wall of China, the most unforgettable pastries and the most rabidly active political parties. Why, we even have the most ridiculously archaic words like 'moral turpitude' in our newspapers. And we also have something more precious than anything money can buy: we have perspective. Being Commie-poor does that to you. You can't really blame us for feeling the rub off like it's a genetic thing. Which is actually very strange, if you work out that we're really quite backward. I mean, we're not street-smart or blasé the way Bombayites are.

What I liked most about Jo was that she epitomized the city. She was sexy, sassy and stimulating. I guess that's because she was brought up in Bombay. She'd only moved to the hostel when her dad retired to some small one-cow town in Uttar Pradesh. She was a total bitch. I mean, while she looked deliciously feminine she could still make men cry for their mothers if they messed with her.

Monica was different. She was a more stolid, earth mother type from stolid, earth mother Chennai. And unbearably pragmatic. I put it down to her being in finance. She was amazingly unflappable too. The only time she lost her cool was while watching Bollywood movies. She detested the fact that molls and easy chicks were given Christian names like Lily and Julie. It really made her bile rise. That's because her mum's Christian, I guess. And, the truth is, she had a valid point. Christians in our country are cruelly typecast as sexually promiscuous. Any good Hindu woman whose husband has a secretary called Mary or something is 99.9 per cent certain that Mary doubles up as a laptop. It's downright unfair.

Both Monica and Jo ditched their dates to be with me and attempted to lift my gloom in their own idiosyncratic ways. Jo offered to introduce me to the men in her office, but I refused. I didn't want to date journalists, especially reporters, not after the time I'd had a drink with this guy who was on the Bombay Municipal Corporation beat. He'd spent the entire night relating what he fondly believed were amusing anecdotes about sewage and other garbage.

'How about the crime beat,' Jo offered hopefully. She came from never-say-die stock.

I turned her down. I like hearing about murders even less than garbage.

'Hey, you know, you're in advertising! Why don't you date some of those hot model types?' Jo persisted.

'The only models I meet are middle-aged losers promoting hair and cooking oils. And besides, what do you say after you say "Hello" to a sexy Dino Morea type? "What toner do you use for open pores"? Nah! No way. No more men for me. I'm going to concentrate on my career now. I'm going to work so hard, I'll be too busy to date. Only thing is, with Super-Bitch Boss around, what career can I have? I mean, the kind of work she gives me, I won't even get ahead of the Xerox-machine boy.'

Monica pulled me up, saying that I was just being negative as usual. That's her pet theme.

'I'm serious, Monica. I spend all my productive hours generating names for dog food and things. It's crap.'

Monica switched the subject to a spot of pop-psychoanalysis. She wanted me to talk about things that I really hated about Low Life. I think she hoped it would bring about emotional catharsis or something. I thought long and hard, but came up with nothing, really. I know lots of women who love their boyfriends without really liking them. They just grimly hang on till someone better comes along. The truth is, no one likes to be alone. But I loved *and* liked Low Life. He was my diametrical opposite, which I found interesting. I'd started being less of a pseud and more open to popular culture in his company. I even saw thriller-type movies, those testosterone-heavy Nicolas Cage ones, and enjoyed them. And—I find this hard to admit—he dared me to read a best-seller (something I'd never have been caught dead with before) and it was just about okay. Not as badly written as I'd imagined it would be.

But Low Life wasn't perfect, which worked because

I'm actually quite fond of flaws. He was alarmingly egotistical. He'd fly into these towering rages when he didn't get his own way and his HR manager had even forced him to attend a course in anger management (didn't help). He wasn't ashamed to be an MCP in an age when advertising too had begun to show men deftly changing nappies and chopping onions. And he was an incurable lech—my god, his head would swivel around like the possessed child in *The Exorcist,* when he was in a room full of chicks. I have this thing for anti-heroes: the less perfect a person is, the more attractive I find him. The first man I fell head over heels in love with was Michael Henchard, the protagonist in Hardy's *The Mayor of Casterbridge.* I mean, this guy sold his wife! He was a domineering, bad-tempered bully and things, but I still saw him as vulnerable and misunderstood. I guess I'm the kind of woman who loves a challenge, who sees herself as being *the one* to tame a maverick. It's an ego thing, I suppose. The only thing I hated about Low Life most then was the fact that he had dumped me. And that he wore socks with his mocs. Very anal, if you ask me. I really should have taken that seriously.

Even so, I hoped like hell that Low Life would call and say he'd made a terrible mistake. But I didn't get lucky. How could I have even expected it when my ruling planet is Saturn, the most relentless taskmaster of all stars? I consoled myself with the thought that he may have been trying and couldn't get through. Our hostel phone lines were always jammed. I guess it's only natural when you live in a post-sexual-revolution city, in close proximity with over a hundred women and their raging hormones. I wished I had a cellphone, but I couldn't afford it. Out of sheer desperation, I almost wished I had a pager at least, even though my image couldn't afford it. Pagers didn't even have status symbol value for plumbers.

And the straw that broke the camel's back was what happened in the dining room that night. Twisted Spinster Warden had evidently heard that I'd been given the old heave-ho. She came up to me, baring her fangs, with her bloody parrot on her shoulder and told it to repeat some shit after her: 'Say "I love you, Arti", say "I love you, Arti".' Fortunately, the parrot remained silent; it was clearly the smarter and more sensitive of the two. The minute she left, I shot up. I must have been green in the face, because Jo looked at me anxiously.

'Where you going?'

'To stab myself in the heart with any sharp object I can lay hands on. Even a toothpick will do.'

'Now what?' she sighed.

'Didn't you just hear what she was teaching the goddamn parrot to say? Twisted Spinster Warden thinks I'm one of them now. God, this is more humiliating than a glitzy "Welcome to the Spinster Club" banner held aloft by over-the-hill cheerleaders. Now I know I'm a total loser.'

It truly was unbearably humiliating, something that called for even deeper and darker music. I listened to Gerry Rafferty's *Baker Street* over and over again to get centred. 'Another year and then you'll be happy,' was the mantra I needed to keep me going. I refused to let Monica and Jo into my room and got down to some serious thinking about my life. I resolved to build a career; that was the only way I'd get to be financially independent. Those days, Dad generously supplemented my pathetically slim pay packet.

As far as emotional independence went, however, I was clueless as to how I should go about it. Low Life had made me soft and needy; I was really frightened I'd never meet anyone again. The thing is I don't make friends easily, thanks to my acid tongue. I'm like an acquired taste or something, not universally appealing like chocolate. Also, I'm not that hot-looking; I'm just about passable, not a *behenji*-type, thank god, but not supermodel material either. That's one of the main reasons I was flattered when Low Life pursued me; the babes he goes for usually top every man's wet-dream list. I asked him about it once in a drunken stupor: why did he choose me? He was really nice about it. He said most hot-looking babes stop being hot once they part their sexy lips to speak, while I was the sort who could pull reasonably intelligent men after I opened my mouth. He still didn't tell me I was pretty or anything, though; guess he was being honest for a change. Hats off to him for that moment of rare candour.

four

My resolutions rarely last longer than a week. That night's had the lifespan of a moth. When I got back to work the next day, I spent all morning concentrating on Low Life's defection instead of my career. Not that I had a career there, not with the kind of Creative Director I had. Super-Bitch Boss always made me wish her mum had been infertile. What I hated most about her was that she gave the plum assignments to guys and us women got stuck with the humdrum chores instead. Tenaz was participating enthusiastically in the grumble, when she suddenly looked up and nudged me. Super-Bitch Boss was summoning us into her den. And her eyes were scrunched up into mean little slits. She looked a bit like how I'd imagine Hitler would have looked when he didn't get his way. I was visibly tense and Tenaz squeezed my hand hard and urged me to relax. 'Hey, chill, her bark is worse than her bite.'

'Don't bet on it,' I warned her. 'You may need fourteen painful shots in your stomach to survive.'

By the time we got into her plush kennel she was

already seated, an icy expression on her face. 'I'm
bombing your ad for Super Woofer. You know why I'm
bombing it?'

'No,' I sighed inwardly. I could feel this big, boring
lecture coming up.

'Because this is a pun, for Chrissake, a pun! The
lowest form of humour!' Her voice rose to a shriek.

I badly wanted to correct her, to tell her that
Shakespeare was the hottest punster of them all, the
pundit of puns in fact—hadn't she read the porter scene
in *Macbeth,* dammit? But I held my tongue. After all, I
knew that I shouldn't make it obvious that I was better
educated than she was. That would have made her feel
threatened and completely ruined whatever I had left of
my career. I can be fairly diplomatic when I choose to.
Which is not very often, actually. Hey, life isn't a popularity
contest.

Super-Bitch Boss fluttered the layout of the ad under
my nose as she pronounced its final death sentence: 'I
wouldn't even use it as toilet paper.' Then, like a magician
pulling a rabbit out of a hat, she whipped out her writing
pad and showed us her scribble. It looked familiar, I'd
definitely seen it before in a *Creative Black Book.* 'Now
this,' she proclaimed triumphantly, 'this is an award-
winner.'

She was right. It was an award-winner; in fact, it had
already won a gold at the Clio Awards three years ago.
The woman was an international idea thief.

Tenaz offered to buy me a cheer-up drink, but I took a rain check because I'd just fixed an appointment with this world-famous-in-Bombay astrologer, a chap Jo had once interviewed. He claimed to be a descendant of Noor Jehan and had invited Jo to his haveli somewhere in Gujarat to show her a few *farmans* that had been issued by his royal ancestor. I thought that was the cheesiest pickup line I'd ever heard. Anyway, apparently he could tell you where to find your stuff if it was stolen or something. I knew where my lost property was, but desperately needed to find out if it would voluntarily come back to me. And *when*, exactly. After all, it was only a matter of time before my collagen collapsed. Those anti-wrinkle ads were really alarming.

I wished I'd asked Tenaz to accompany me when I reached the astrologer's place. It was horribly grungy, with the stench of incense hanging heavy in the air. I really dislike the smell of incense. It's overpoweringly cloying, infinitely worse than being in a ten-person-capacity elevator packed with thirty-six sweaty people. The entrance was swarming with depressed people who looked like they had far better reasons than I to hang themselves from ceiling fans. I was relieved when my turn came. I was escorted to this tiny, dimly-lit room and given what clearly looked like a bug-infested chair to sit on. I opted to stand. Not that it would have mattered if I'd sat down anyway. Lice tend to scurry away from me. Take Low Life, for example.

I discovered that I'd squandered mega bucks to hear things I knew already. Like Low Life not being in my stars. When I asked the astrologer if I'd ever get married to anyone at all, he averted his eyes (the coward) and told me to come back and see him next year. I knew what that meant: I was going to spend the rest of my life with a parrot as a live-in companion. And with my kind of luck, it would probably be the female of the species. That really shook me up. What twisted the knife in the wound was that the astrologer didn't invite me to his palatial home to admire Noor Jehan's *farmans*. I was such a loser, even *he* didn't want me.

Jo had a surprise waiting for me when I returned to the hostel after my unrewarding astrology session. 'Kindly find enclosed your transition man,' she trilled as she handed me this gaily-wrapped package.

'Ooh, he's better-looking than Low Life,' I jibed, when I unwrapped the 'Made in Taiwan' sexual-gratification gizmo. These thingies were easily available on the busy, bustling pavements next to Flora Fountain (Bombay's starchy business district, if you please) and they sold like hot *vada paos*.

Jo looked smugly pleased, like she'd given me Keanu Reeves or something. She pointed to the five-year guarantee card. 'And look, it's guaranteed to last longer than a relationship with a man.'

'Hallelujah. Nonetheless, Jo, I can't use it. It'll be like rubbing salt into the womb.'

Jo eyed me critically. 'You know what you desperately need? A haircut.'

'Why, is my hair looking like shit?'

'No, but a new hairstyle is the best cure for depression. Even better than new shoes.'

'Don't knock new shoes, dahlink,' I wagged a finger at her. 'The next pair I'm going to buy will have razor-sharp stiletto heels. All the better to walk over men with!'

Suddenly I heard my name being hollered. 'Arti! Arti! Goddammit, Arti! Call for you.'

I felt butterflies doing cartwheels in my tummy. It had to be Low Life. It just had to be, begging for forgiveness, was what I thought. Jo must have seen the flicker of hope in my eyes (she's sharp, that one, she doesn't miss a trick) and she stared thoughtfully at me. I knew what she was thinking: Low Life whistles and Arti goes bounding back. And maybe she was right. I was a total sucker for him. One of those wimpy, hopelessly-devoted-to-you, whistle-and-I'll-come-running types. Monica used to contemptuously say that I was suffering from Stockholm syndrome.

I picked up the receiver tentatively, praying that my voice would remain steady. I needn't have bothered, because it was Mum. She'd heard about my break-up and had already gone through the national census data to find a husband for me. I told you, that woman's a superpower in her own right.

'Give me a break, Ma! I need time to get over Sandy.'

Mum snorted contemptuously. 'You're too old for this get-over nonsense. Just meet this man. He's arty like you, Arti. He's a wildlife photographer. You'll like him.'

'If he's so hot, why does he have to advertise for a wife?' I argued.

'If you think you're so hot, how come you're not married yet?' My god, she really knew how to rub it in.

'That's right, hit below the belt. You sure you're not my evil stepmum?' Totally screwed as usual, I hit the bottle of cough syrup the instant I returned to the room.

Jo winced; she hated that bottle with a passion. 'It was the cretin, right?'

'I'd be popping open a bottle of champagne if it was. Nah, it was Mum. She's trying to fix me up, as usual.'

'What's wrong with meeting someone? You can always say no if you don't like him.'

'Bullshit. This arranged marriage thing won't work. I'll be divorced on my wedding night when he discovers I'm not a virgin. You know what Indian men are like.' I'd taken such a deep swig of the cough syrup, it was already dancing through my veins. I felt so light-headed, I burst into a parody of a song from *Grease*: 'Sandy, can't you see I'm in misery, you stole my cherry and it won't come back to me. My hymen's torn, I'm divorced and alone and I sit and wonder why-y-y, oh why you left me, oh Sandy . . .'

Jo ignored my mad caper and focussed on a solution. She looked dead serious too. 'Rubbish. All you have to do is scream when you do it.'

'What? Just a few yells will do the trick?' I couldn't believe she was serious.

'No, you've got to really feel it.'

'Like, how?' I looked at her like she was suffering from mad cow disease or something.

Jo looked smug, very, very smug indeed, as she delivered her punchline. 'Superglue yourself down there.'

'*Ouch*! Gross!'

'The point is, it will work.'

'The point is, divorce is less painful,' I informed her dryly.

I turned my back on her indicating that the subject was closed and started rifling through my tapes. What I wanted to listen to right then was Joan Baez's cynical *Love song to a stranger*. It seemed kind of appropriate at the moment. Typically, the first cassette my hand fell on was something Low Life had compiled for me. It was mainly full of schmaltzy, saccharine Air Supply and Boy Zone shit—stuff that could send diabetics into an instant coma. The only song I liked was Police's *Every breath you take*. I don't know why, I just did. Also the fact that it was our song kind of helped; we'd always clung to each other when it played.

I cold-bloodedly chucked it into the bin and Jo looked up, interested. 'What's that?'

'Some Air Supply crap Low Life gave me when we'd started dating.'

'Yuck! I thought he had good taste in music!' Jo looked like she desperately needed a barf bag.

'He does. He just thinks chicks undress faster with that kind of sickly stuff.'

'Hey, didn't you tell me his dad went bald at age thirty-four?'

'What's that got to do with … oh, right, it's hereditary. Low Life's got just one year to do a Yul Brynner. Hooray!'

Jo knew exactly how to cheer me up. If she were a man, I'd probably have dumped Low Life for her. Really. We hung out on my little veranda and waved to Monica as she got into Dev's car. The lucky bitch was going to be wined and dined. Jo's face darkened when the car drove away.

'I don't know what she sees in that two-timing bastard.'

'Let her be. She's not a fool.'

'Yeah, I guess,' Jo agreed grudgingly.

'You know, when it comes to men, even smart women act dumb.'

Jo sighed deeply, 'You can say that again.'

'Okay. When it comes to men, even smart women act dumb.'

Jo gave me a push and I pushed her back. We had fun shooting the breeze that night, bitching out men. I'm a moderate feminist, not the burn-the-bra type. That's dumb—you'll only sag. But I enjoy a bit of male-bashing now and then, especially then, when the male being bashed was Low Life. That evening, I'd have loved a dartboard with his mugshot in the bullseye circle. It was way high on my wish list. I even foolishly thought the healing process had begun. I mean, I could laugh at him, that was a bloody start.

five

I was serious about what I'd said to Jo, though: 'When it comes to men, even smart women act dumb.' It was my turn to prove the theory right and I did it the very next day. I'd had a gruelling time at work; Murphy's Law was in action. Super-Bitch Boss snarled at me the entire day and I had to bite back the urge to tell her, 'Roll over and play dead, bitch.' Self-pity leads to tempting thoughts of suicide as we all know, and the stage was set for my intellectual *harakiri*. Tenaz and I had knocked back a couple of quick stiff ones to recover from Super-Bitch Boss's venomous attacks, and then she had to dash off for a date with her neighbour of all people, she was that desperate for male attention. I was at a loose end, and there are no prizes for guessing where I landed up in my alcoholic haze. Yup, Low Life's apartment, just like a homing pigeon, ignoring my eviction notice. I vaguely remember humming *Whisky bar* in a happy sort of way. I was sure he'd take me back.

I must have rung the bell at least fifteen times before Low Life opened the door. His jaw practically scraped the floor when he saw me slumped against the wall. I cheerfully slurred, 'Donsh wansh to gesh marriedsh. Wansh you backsh inshtead.'

He contemplated me in unsmiling silence. I slumped against the wall again, willing to wait that one out. The silence was broken by hurried footsteps. Bimbo Dogess, wearing nothing but one of Low Life's tees (to add insult to injury, one I'd given him), came pounding to the door. She blanched when she saw me. This is when I should have turned tail and run, but I had enough Dutch courage to take on the Mossad and the Shiv Sena combined that night; a floozie seemed like easy meat. Especially one who looked as though the only sentence she could quote from literature was, 'The cat sat on the mat.'

She was street-smart though, something I'm not. Even my algebra's better. She looked Low Life in the eye and said, 'Either she gets out right now or I do.'

Low Life looked at me pleadingly. I crossed my arms mutinously. He mumbled, 'You'd better go.'

I felt like a jug of ice-cold water had been poured down my back and sobered up instantly. I left without looking back and flinched when I heard the door slam shut. The lily-livered coward did it real quick. I could swear I heard bolts and chains being drawn too, just in case I returned with a hatchet.

One and a half bottles of cough syrup were drained

that night. I could have had more, but I ran out, that's
how mortified I was. Jo and Monica were real bricks,
though. They didn't get all judgemental on me, just
heard me out and said a few 'there, theres'. Of course,
Monica couldn't resist adding that I could have won the
direct opposite of a Mensa award that night. But she said
it affectionately, not in a rub-it-in kind of way. I begged
them for alone-time; I desperately needed to lick my
wounds in private. They departed reluctantly.

As the strains of King Crimson's deeply pessimistic
Epitaph washed over the room, I mentally kicked myself
again and again for my stupidity. I think I had dozed off
for a few minutes when dawn was beginning to break,
and woke up screaming. I had this nightmare in which
I was running my fingers through Low Life's hair and
bright green feathers came off in my hand. Guess Freud
would say that was my acceptance of the fact that I'd
spend the rest of my life with a bloody parrot. Cripes,
I still break into a cold sweat when I remember that
creepy nightmare. It's worse than the one I had as a
child, when I dreamed that a charred hand emerged
from a funeral pyre and yanked me in.

Anyway, I was too ill to go to work the next day. Jo
found me clutching my head. Honestly, it felt like a
million carpenters were hammering and drilling inside.
She forced me to join her for breakfast but the smell of
frying eggs made me retch. I raced to the loo and threw

up violently. At least six times. I was tucked into bed with an anti-nausea tab and a few backdated issues of *Cosmo*. I weakly flipped through them and read 'How to Tell If a Guy Is Cheating on You' for future reference. After going through all three of them I discovered that to attract a man all you have to do is wear lacy black or fire-engine red undies and teddies. What I didn't understand was, were we supposed to wear them on top of our clothes like Superman? Or strip the minute we were introduced to a hunk and say, 'Ready, teddy, go!' Or modestly carry a placard saying, 'Am wearing red lacy undies.' I made a mental note to write a letter to the *Cosmo* ed. to find out. I probably would have done it there and then, if I wasn't feeling so wasted. I had to conserve all my energy for frequent up-chucking trips.

Monica returned to find me with my head down the potty again and whisked me away to a doctor despite my protestations. I was too weak to argue. I almost threw up on the doctor's pristine white lab jacket when she plunged an ice lolly kind of stick down my throat. In retrospect, I wish I'd done that. She was a totally unsympathetic bitch. After a brief examination, she indicated a little curtained-off area and asked me to drop my trousers. I staunchly refused and hissed in Monica's ear.

'Let's get out of here fast! Race you to the door, she's a bloody lesbian.'

'Don't be a fool, Arti! Just do as she says.'

'No fucking way! I mean, I've heard of weird remedies for hangovers before, like putting a frog on your head, but this one takes the cake.'

Monica dragged me aside. Her face looked pinched and she broke the news to me as gently as anyone of her calibre could. 'She thinks you may be pregnant, dammit.'

I keeled over. When I came to, I was being body-searched in a particularly unpleasant and undignified way. Fabulous. I remember bitterly thinking that this was probably the last time in the world I would be felt up and it had to be by a woman. That's the problem with me. Even when life shits on me, I think of inconsequential things first. Maybe I'm shallow.

Back at the hostel, however, reality bit. Real hard. Monica, Jo and I tried to work out a game plan in an atmosphere of gloom and doom. There wasn't even a drop of cough syrup left to numb my pain and both of them refused to buy me one. Jo thoughtfully added that it might harm the baby. She also suggested that I tell Low Life about it. That wasn't an option, as far as I was concerned. The 'Honey, I'm pregnant' line wasn't going to make his eyes light up with joy, of that I was certain. 'Forget it, Jo. At best, he'd offer to split the abortion bill with me.'

'You're not going to have it aborted!' Jo gasped.

I nodded vehemently. 'Of course I am. I *definitely* don't want it and my parents will kill me if I keep it.'

Monica put in her two-pice bit. 'Not necessarily, Arti. Six out of ten parents forgive their unmarried daughters for having babies.'

'Mine are the four out of ten,' I added glumly. 'My mum will slit my throat if I have it.'

But even as I contemplated the abortion (hell, it was the only way out; apart from the burning shame, I wasn't earning enough to support myself, how could I support a baby?) I felt queasy. I didn't know if I could live with it. Suicide seemed the only way out. That way, I wouldn't have to live with any decision. I could buy a hundred bottles of cough syrup and OD myself to a blissful death, I thought. I still wasn't sure, though. Suicide stank. It was the loser's way out. Also, I didn't want to be reborn as a poor, uneducated sod in a village without electricity and water as punishment for terminating my life. This life was lousy enough already. What I privately tried to figure out was whether I was mentally and emotionally strong enough to give birth to a metaphorical bastard's bastard child. Honestly, I still don't know the answer to that one.

We kept an all-night vigil with Jo adding reassuringly every now and then that the pee test results were yet to come in, while Monica determinedly flipped through the Yellow Pages for abortion clinics. None of us trusted

Sapphire Abortion Centre at Mulund, even though each and every compartment in each and every one of Bombay's commuter trains had a tin plate advertising their cheap, seventy-rupee instant abortion services. We suspected they used bludgeons instead of anaesthesia and unsterilized hangers as surgical equipment. I knew one thing for certain that night: if there was a god, he really hated me. Much, much more than Super-Bitch Boss did. I really feel uncomfortable talking about that night. All I can say is, I've never felt so alone, bewildered and terrifyingly helpless before or after. It's something I wish I could delete from my memory forever.

The next day, all three of us arrived at the Bitch Doctor's chambers long before the cleaning lady did. Jo went through my horoscope in about eight mags and all of them said more or less the same thing: I'd get joyful news. Even Ma Prem Usha, my favourite Osho tarot-card reader, said the same and she's usually right. Jo thought that ought to cheer me up, but it had the opposite effect.

'Yeah, Jo, tell me about it. That's the line we use in ads when the wife coyly tells her husband that she's pregnant.'

We slumped in gloom again till the Bitch Doctor arrived and summoned me in. I could tell that she wanted to make me wait (she thought I was a cheap slut or something), but couldn't since I was, officially, the first patient.

When I emerged from her room, Monica and Jo were looking pale. Tension, evidently, is far more effective than a skin-whitening cream. I let them sweat it out a bit more—it was clearly good for their complexions—and then let out a whoop of joy.

'I *told* you she was a lesbian!' I loudly hissed to Monica and noticed the other patients cringe. A few of the women scurried out. Not that I cared; the Bitch Doctor had lousy bedside manners, she deserved to lose patients. We got into a hug-huddle and it was then that I decided that in future, I'd lay off the freebie snacks at cheap bars. After all, food poisoning can be very traumatic. More important, instead of keeping my fingers crossed, I'd keep my thighs crossed. Sex can be alarmingly fattening. It thickens the waistline long before middle age does.

six

What annoyed me most about Super-Bitch Boss was that she made damn well sure we couldn't ever go out for a breather during the lunch break. She'd dump a 3 p.m. deadline on us at, like, 12.55 p.m. and dash off to a five-star restaurant for cocktails and a fancy meal on a client's expense account. When she'd return, she'd crack the whip for the rest of the day. That woman could get belligerent just by sniffing alcohol, it's clear she came from vulgar, pub-brawl stock. She did that to me again that day, and nuked my plans of having a freebie lunch at a new seafood restaurant specializing in fancy fusion cuisine that Jo was reviewing for her food column.

I had to settle for my usual boring, calorie-rich cheese toast from the office canteen instead. Tenaz joined me with her usual: a low-fat, egg-white salad from home. She eyed my cheese toast with distaste and told me my body desperately needed a bit of sculpting.

'Hello! Do I look like the Good Year blimp or something?' I was horrified.

'Relax, you're just borderline, nothing that a few aerobic sessions can't cure,' she said reassuringly, but I was hyperventilating already. It was bad enough being single, but being single and frumpy was horrifying.

I immediately resolved to exercise, but scrapped the idea of aerobics, because the first and last time I'd tried it, I almost required an ambulance service to get home, my muscles were that stiff! Also, I totally detest that cheap disco music they play. I mean, rock has some sexy, adrenaline-pumping numbers like Deep Purple's *Highway star*; stuff like that can even make the Energizer Bunny pant and wheeze, why can't they play decent music like that, dammit? Tenaz suggested yoga instead. That appealed to me. It was just what the doctor ordered to keep my mind relaxed and my body supple. I even fleetingly hoped that yoga might entice Low Life back into my ever-lovin', newly-toned arms again. But stuff like that only happens in TV commercials. I know, I used to write that crap.

I called a phone service for details of the yoga centre and fixed up my first class for that evening. I was really looking forward to it. In fact, I kind of imagined that my instructor would be a celebrated Maharishi—Mahayogi type, the chap who taught the Beatles and sundry other celebrities. I was deeply disappointed when I met Swamiji. Despite the fact that he had a calming countenance and a phlegmatic, other-worldly smile like most Amar Chitra Katha rishis, he looked like he couldn't teach anyone anything. I mean, he was way too laid-back. I lost confidence in him when he uttered his first sentence. 'Can you breathe, madam?' he asked in a gentle voice.

I gazed at him with contempt, like he was a village idiot or something. After all, he'd seen me arrive in a cab, not a hearse. Before I could make a scathing remark, he'd started doing this heavy-duty panting routine. Sort of like a thirsty dog racing through a desert at high noon. He sounded remarkably like the heavy breather who called the hostel every night at 11 p.m. on the dot, without fail. While I looked at Swamiji with new interest, wondering if that pervert was really him, he cut into my musings and explained that that's all I needed to do to detox myself. That's when I realized to my horror that I'd been breathing wrong all my life. I wondered how I'd lived for so long, but Swamiji reassured me that he'd teach me in a few months. I was certain I'd die of carbon monoxide poisoning before then. I really didn't need this new addition to my already long list of neuroses. If I'd been an American, I'd have sued him big time for that.

What I really wanted to learn was to meditate though, to blank Low Life out of my mind, the sod kept creeping in uninvited. Swamiji obligingly demonstrated the lotus posture. I tried to imitate him, but my legs refused to lock into place and my bones creaked like a rusted gate. Tenaz was right. I was hopelessly out of shape. She'd warned me that if I didn't get my act together fast, I'd probably find even the missionary position difficult to execute if ever I got lucky again. Swamiji finally yanked my legs into position. Bloody uncomfortable it was too. All I could concentrate on initially was the pain. And then, suddenly, my mind lifted on its own accord and I got this technicolour vision: Low Life and Bimbo Dogess necking in slow motion. I leapt up and told Swamiji that this yoga thingie wasn't working for me, but he urged me to try out a few more classes first. After all, I'd already coughed up fees for a month, he reminded me, gently implying that there was no way in hell he was giving it back. He said this with his usual non-materialistic, other-worldly smile, of course. He was right. That was one good reason to pursue it, I thought. Another more frivolous one that crept into my mind was that if I got really good at it, I could open an ashram and teach rock stars who would buy me stretch limos and worship me in return. Hell, even if they didn't buy me fancy cars, I'd still have raked in a darn sight more than what I was earning back then. But you know, I tried the meditation thingie in my room the next morning and I got that picture of Low Life and Bimbo Dogess in my head again. It killed me. I never went back. I'm not a masochist.

If Confucius were in advertising, I bet he'd say, 'When wliting dull packaging copy, intelluptions are walmly welcomed.' I got a phone call the next day while I was getting positively hyperbolic about the vitamin-enriched properties of an oat-based breakfast cereal. One that the client privately confessed he wouldn't even feed to his horse. It truly was a cereal killer. I snatched the receiver from Tenaz's hand like it was a lifesaver or something. I got even more excited when Tenaz whispered that it was a male with a sexy voice, the kind you associate with Lamborghini owners. It turned out to be Mum's wildlife photographer, the wimp from the matrimonial ad. I resisted the urge to turn him down. That would have made Mum unbearably aggro. We arranged to meet at 7 p.m. that night in the Taj Hotel lobby, every hostelite's favourite hang-out joint. On hot summer Sundays and holidays, Monica, Jo and I would lounge around there for hours, reading or listening to music on our Walkmans in air-conditioned comfort. You'd just have to glance impatiently at your watch now and then, pretending you were waiting for someone, when the hotel staff walked past. They were pretty cool, actually.

The wildlife chap agreed. He said we could probably go to one of the hotel's bars. I decided to check out his humour index and asked if I should carry a red and white cane as identification; after all, it was technically a blind date. There was this long pause followed by a Big

Moose-like 'Duh'. Oh well, I consoled myself, at least I wouldn't have to eat recycled garbage at the hostel for dinner.

I hung up and immersed myself in the packaging copy. Tenaz leaned over my shoulder and instructed me to keep it short—she'd set aside limited space for it in her layout.

'You art guys are all the same. You think copy is, like, an unnecessary evil or something. Quick, gimme some superlatives for "best",' I beseeched her.

'Bestest,' was all Tenaz could offer, after scratching her head.

I winced and was about to launch into a tirade on Bombay's deplorable standards of education, when this hunk of manhood walked into our cubicle. Admittedly, he wasn't exactly a Greek god or a Hollywood star clone, not even close, but he had an interesting face and exuded enough SA to send Tenaz into a dizzy tizzy. As he introduced himself to us, I noticed an unbecoming flush on Tenaz's cheeks, like she was going through premature menopause or something.

'Hi! I'm Aditya, the new accounts supe on Household Cleaning Products. The Creative Director asked me to brief the two of you on a small job.'

I introduced myself and had to introduce Tenaz too, because she was hopelessly tongue-tied. 'So what does the bitch want us to do this time? Create an ad for the back of bus tickets, telling maids to sack their memsaabs if they don't buy our client's shitty products?' I asked sarcastically.

He grinned and assured me that it was a little more mentally stimulating than that. He'd be back with the brief shortly, he said. At least he had a sense of humour.

The minute New Guy left, Tenaz got her power of speech back. She sighed deeply in a multiple-orgasmic sort of way and swore she'd get to know him better.

'You mean in the biblical sense?' I asked, surprised. I mean, he wasn't *that* hot.

'Yes, oh yes,' she moaned in reply.

In that case, I told her, she'd better enrol for classes in sign language, the way she was going, he'd think she was vocally-challenged. Tenaz was too high on pheromones to take umbrage at that. She just smiled dreamily while mentally working out her MO to ensnare New Guy. I discovered later, when we eventually got the brief, that Tenaz was pretty accomplished at come-on vibes. She had New Guy literally eating out of her hand and he even accepted her offer of a let-me-debrief-you-on-the-agency drink that evening. I think he cottoned on that what she really meant was just 'Let me debrief you'. Men can't resist that sort of thing. They're shameless opportunists.

'Fast work,' I congratulated her, when we got back to our cubicle.

She raised her eyebrows archly at me. 'Thanks to you. You make me realize I'm running out of time every time you bring up those dumb, anti-wrinkle cream ads.'

'Hey, hey, they can be pretty frightening!' I defended myself.

Both of us picked up our bags and made a beeline for the loo to tart up for our respective dates. I didn't have time to change for the meeting with the wildlife photographer. Not that I cared. I was determined to reject him. Tenaz was laying on the warpaint real thick, though. Sky-high cheekbones were created with blush-on. Her eyes suddenly became almond-shaped with the help of eyeliner and she even tried to change the shape of her nose till I warned her that New Guy might not recognize her when she stepped out.

My knees turned to jelly when I alighted from the cab at the Taj. I've never been good at PC and I was straining my brain trying to figure out what I could talk to this stranger about: the state of the nation? Brad Pitt's highly-publicized dandruff problem? Are meerkats and domestic tabbies third cousins? I tried to remember all the wildlife programmes I'd seen on Nat. Geo., but my mind was a blank. Honestly, all I could think of was a question that used to bother me a lot: why are wildlife cameramen so obsessed with animals making out? Not exactly the stuff that's politically correct to bring up at an arranged-marriage date.

I recognized him instantly. Not because I'm clairvoyant, but because he was the only male reading a magazine with a herd of wildebeest on the cover. God, I badly needed Dutch courage to loosen up. I gave him a tight smile and hastily ordered an XXL shot of rum before the waiter even handed us the wine list at the bar. It was only after the first sip that I really looked at him, and I have to confess that I rated him a seven on ten. He was nice-looking in a rugged sort of way, deeply tanned a delicious red-brown, with glints of gold shining through his stubble. Much better-looking than Low Life. Really, most non-corporate-looking men are easier on the eye. And I was turned on by the rich texture of his voice. Just when we were getting along pretty famously and I was mentally congratulating Mum on her choice in men, the glitch appeared.

'The truth is, I find real jungles more peaceful than concrete ones like Bombay,' he said.

'So which animals do you like shooting best?' I ventured.

'The big cats. Tigers, leopards and loins.'

I was sure I'd misheard him, so I asked him to repeat the sentence. He said 'loins' instead of 'lions' again. My heart sank. I'm way too much of an intellectual snob to let such a glaring pronunciation howler pass. I asked for the bill and dashed out of there really fast. He insisted we meet again, but I fobbed him off ruthlessly. Hell, I was sure of one thing: I'd rather die a tragic Miss Havisham than spend the rest of my life with a man who shoots goddamn loins. Honestly, he sounded more like a porn photographer than a wildlife chap.

seven

By the time I returned to the hostel, I'd resigned myself to the fact that many moons could pass before I went on a honeymoon. After hitting the cough-syrup bottle, I liberally applied anti-cellulite cream on my thighs. They were okay at that point in time, but I had to keep them in pristine condition in case I got lucky only after I was 100 years old or something. Monica walked in and sneered at my paranoia. She's not very sympathetic, in case you haven't noticed. The biggest problem with finance people is that they don't have imagination; they just can't see ahead. I'm willing to lay a bet that all the people you see with wrinkles on their faces and chicken necks at age forty have calculators instead of brains.

After a couple of hours, Jo wafted in with her ring finger in upright position. It looked extremely vulgar and both Monica and I wondered aloud why she was being rude to us. We were condemned as philistines as Jo dramatically held her finger up to the light and we were dazzled by the sparkle.

'Congratulate me, bitches. I'm engaged.'

'What? Your Lust Bug finally gave in?' Monica said, looking mildly surprised.

'Not finally. Willingly,' Jo hastened to assure her. Then added, 'Pretty impressive, isn't it?'

'Looks more like a chip off the old block to me,' I grudgingly intoned as I hugged her.

'Sweetie, you just have a massive chip on your frail shoulders,' Jo sang gaily.

I was in a state of shock. Hell, this was a revelation to me! I'd thought all single men who didn't circle matrimonial ads were rabid commitment-phobes. My opinion of Lust Bug shot up several notches. 'Lissen Jo, if he has a twin, I bag him first,' I hastily put in, before Monica could appropriate the rights.

'Nope, no twin, but a friend in software who, I think, would meet with your approval,' Jo generously offered.

'Bring on the software chap then,' I pleaded. 'Chances are, you have a better understanding of my taste in men than Mum.'

I was right. Jo did know the kind of guys I went for. Software was hot shit. I met him at a cosy foursome Jo organized at a pub about a week later. He wasn't tall. Not dark. And definitely not handsome. But he was the ultimate in cool and had a fantastic sense of humour. I mean, he could even quote effortlessly from Mel Brooks movies; more of a turn-on than a bloody Shakespearean sonnet, and he had me thinking, 'Hey, where has this guy been all my life?' You know, guys from top-notch engineering institutes are actually more interesting than non-engineering types. They're dismissed as geeks, but they're way cooler. The left and right sides of their brains are equally developed and they know everything about everything. I mean, we think they spend their time swotting $e=mc^2$ stuff, but they're actually getting stoned and doing dissertations on Jim Morrison and Ravi Shankar and things just for fun. And they know stuff like Hendrix's fender stratocaster was called Black Beauty and they almost always own great, hard-to-acquire music like John Dummer and the Ooblee Dooblee Band. When it comes to bodies too, theirs are perfectly toned and muscular, thanks to the mandatory tennis and squash courts on campus. I find them irresistible.

I nodded my appreciation when he went to the bar with Lust Bug to replenish our drinks. Jo looked as pleased as Punch. 'Maybe he'll help you get over Low Life,' she said.

That depressed me. I mean, this guy was definitely smarter than Low Life. Even his repertoire of jokes went way beyond Low Life's tired and derivative, 'There was an Irishman, an Englishman and a Jew' ice-breakers, but I still yearned for the bastard. I deftly changed the subject. 'I met a headhunter today. I've decided to cut loose from Super-Bitch Boss.'

'Why don't you give journalism a shot too? You're a good writer.'

'Nope, advertising has more substance than journalism,' I loftily told her, and pointed out, 'haven't you noticed, more used sanitary napkins are wrapped in editorials than ads?' Jo tried to argue with me, but I silenced her. 'Face it, Jo. Editorials don't come with valuable price-off coupons.'

The guys rejoined us before Jo could unsheathe her claws. I was so delightfully witty for the rest of the evening, Software would have asked me out on a private date even if I'd looked like (and weighed as much as) Margaret Thatcher on a bad-hair day. I was the queen of stand-up. I returned to the hostel, high on booze and soaring on confidence. I had a real McCoy date pencilled into my little black book for the next week, a 20/20 vision date as opposed to Mum's blind dates, dammit.

I went to office the next day, floating on cloud nine. Super-Bitch Boss swiftly brought me back to earth with a thud—she gave me a rush-rush assignment that kept me working long after the dinner service at the hostel ended. Tenaz had been as grouchy as a bear with a sore head all day. I gathered that either she'd had a tiff with New Guy or that her seduction moves weren't going according to plan. She refused to discuss it, however, something that I found very strange. The fact is, women are more kiss-and-tell than men. And men know that, I think. I guess that's why they're always wary of their girlfriends' best friends. They're totally paranoid about whether the best friends know about the night even a truckload of Viagra failed them. The poor things can't even fake it and then they have the gall to call us the second sex. Sour grapes, that's what.

Anyway, I was way too busy to wheedle secrets out of her and was crouched over my PC, silently cursing the office admin staff for not getting ergonomically-designed chairs. My neck was aching. All I was yearning for right then was an anti-inflammatory tablet and bed. I'd even have traded my date with Software for that, the pain was that excruciating. New Guy came up to me at about 11 p.m. It was his job we were burning the midnight oil for and he wanted to make sure his slaves were whistling merrily while they worked like Snow White's dwarves. 'Can I get you a coffee?' he asked solicitously.

'I'd prefer traction instead. Can you arrange for a physiotherapist at short notice?' I was massaging my neck as I spoke and New Guy offered to ease my pain.

'Here, let me give you a therapeutic massage.'

I demurred. After all, I barely knew him well enough to borrow his gold-plated Cross pen to sign a cheque. How could I borrow his hands to knead my vertebrae? Also, I'd been untouched by a man for so long, there was more than a slim chance that even the most innocuous physical contact would inspire me to rush for a cold shower. New Guy, however, ignored my coy rejection and plunged in. I must say he was the best hands-on

person I'd experienced. He was really good and after the
first few seconds, I felt the knot at the base of my neck
dissolve. I was so grateful, I offered to polish his shoes
and butter his toasts for a month. 'Tell all to mother, were
you a Thai masseuse in your past life?' I gushed gratefully.

I couldn't see his face since he was still massaging my
neck, but I could swear his eyes twinkled at that. 'Actually,
I'm an excellent thigh masseuse in this life too. Er, the
anatomy, not the country. Should I demonstrate?' He
wickedly put his hand on my thigh and just then (I *told*
you I have fucked luck). Tenaz walked in from the studio.
Her eyeballs almost leapt out of their sockets and the
look she skewered me with was more spine-chilling
than anything I'd got from Super-Bitch Boss. I stiffened,
but New Guy wasn't put out a bit. He grinned cheesily
at Tenaz and offered to make her moan with pleasure
too. That mollified her a bit and she gamely thrust out
her thighs. But the spell was broken and after a few
avuncular pats, he returned to his cabin.

Tenaz's smile vanished the minute he turned the
corner. 'What was that all about?' she ground out through
gritted teeth. I shrugged. I wasn't going to waste my time
explaining my innocence to someone who foolishly
thought that the person she had the hots for was
everybody's dream guy. I, after all, had much bigger
dreams. And I kind of hoped Software would star in my
I-want-to-make-it-with-you fantasy.

eight

You know that song *Substitute* by The Who? The one that goes, 'I was born with a plastic spoon in my mouth'? It could have been written for me. I honestly believe that god ran out of silver spoons when it came to my turn. Even the next best stainless steel ones were, evidently, out of stock.

I had the oddest time imaginable with Software, starting from our first official date. Software arrived at the hostel looking all hot and bothered and said we couldn't go out because his car had started acting up. So he suggested we chat there instead. I felt grossly overdressed. After all, I had anticipated a night on the town, not in the fucking hostel lounge under Twisted Spinster Warden's beaky nose. I caught her giving me a stern, we-don't-want-any-goings-on-here glare. Hell, I couldn't really blame her, because emerald-green eyeshadow only looks magical in softly-glowing lamplight. Under the harsh glare of 1000 watt arrest-the-couple-necking-in-the-corner neon lights, it made me look like a cheap Bollywood cabaret artiste called

Mona Darling. Also, the slit in the Suzie Wong dress I'd borrowed from Jo went all the way up my thigh and I had to surreptitiously pinch the two ends together to protect myself from the salacious stares of other male visitors and the hostel staff.

After about fifteen minutes of squirming uncomfortably, I suggested we move to a nearby park instead. Thankfully he agreed, and I dashed up and changed into suitable gear. Once we were away from prying eyes I began to relax, despite the fact that the park watchmen would flash their torches at us suspiciously now and then. I had a vastly entertaining time discussing books, music and suchlike, till hunger pangs made their presence felt.

I suggested we grab a bite, but he said he wasn't hungry. In fact, he added, he was used to going through long periods without food. Just when I was bitterly thinking he must have been a camel in his last life, he gallantly remarked that looking at me was enough to satisfy his appetite. While I was flattered, I was also disappointed. A girl can't live on love and fresh air alone. She needs proteins and carbohydrates too, and chocolate mousse to top it off. Anyway, I didn't pursue the dinner angle since he obviously wasn't interested in watching me masticate.

Software must have seen the naked hunger lurking in my eyes because a short while later he suggested we grab a bite at a little cafe just outside the park that specialized in South Indian snacks. That was not an option, as far as I was concerned. I mean, get real, idlis and chutney are not conducive to love, they're way down in my list of aphrodisiacs. They're what married, heavily-mortgaged couples dine on, since they're too broke for anything better. It was far better to eat the crappy hostel dinner, so I called it a night at 9.45 p.m. I was too late: the dining room was locked by the time I returned. I rushed to Monica's room (Jo was romancing Lust Bug) for sustenance. All she could offer me were a few mouldy old biscuits and the dregs of a jar of mango pickle. I was so hungry, I would have happily eaten paper with a dash of salt. Monica was at her starchy best, however. She thought the whole affair was very strange and didn't buy the 'car has started acting up' line. Her take was that Software had either been pink-slipped or he was just plain cheap.

I hotly defended him and went back to my room, brushing over his oddness and gloating over the romantic sweet nothings he'd whispered in my ear. I found myself comparing him with Low Life. While Low Life scored higher in the hunk department, Software was a hands-down winner as far as grey matter went. I can bet my last buck that the most deep and meaningful book Low Life's read (till date) is *Noddy and Big Ears Throw a Party*, and I realized to my horror that the only author he

could quote was Harold Robbins. Honestly, that night I
wanted to kick myself for not dumping him first.

As I tucked myself into bed, I realized that Software
hadn't attempted to do anything unprintable. He hadn't
even held my moist-with-anticipation hand. Perhaps, I
thought to myself, I'd finally met a gentleman.

He called bright and early the next morning, saying
that he'd pick me up from the office after work. I
fervently hoped we'd go out some place this time,
because I didn't exactly fancy playing footsie under the
receptionist's desk. I sang tunelessly while bathing and
dour Monica wanted to know what I was so happy
about. I told her, and she warned me to have a heavy
Gujarati thali lunch and to slip a few packs of chips into
my bag just in case he claimed that a pickpocket had
pinched his wallet.

'God, Monica, do you have to be cynical all the
fucking time?' I admonished her.

It was a crazy day at work. I thought I might have to
cancel the date, but I slaved like a dog and managed to
fill the out tray. The thing is, I work best under pressure.
Not pressure from Super-Bitch Boss, but from young,
hot-blooded males with a sense of humour. I freshened
up in the loo and got a wolf whistle when I emerged,
but since it was only from Tenaz I discounted it. She'd
forgiven me for my little massage from New Guy after
she discovered me scribbling Software's name on my

writing pad about a zillion times. In flowery, girlie handwriting too. My god, I had a teenage-type crush on him. I mean, if he'd held my hand I probably wouldn't have washed it for weeks or something.

I was so happy to see Software, I fell into his arms like a ripe plum. He told me he was taking me to a very special place and I had visions of a swanky joint where the wine list didn't include a section on domestic spirits. I was mentally tossing up between a Kahlua-based cocktail and Stolichnaya on the rocks when I realized that we were parked at Marine Drive. I thought he'd stopped to get fags or something, but he switched off the engine and gave me a let-the-games-begin smile.

That guy was the most impecunious dotcommer I'd ever met. I mean, while I *love* walks down Marine Drive in the rain, this is the sort of place where cash-strapped maids and drivers woo each other and make out. People like us don't neck there. I tried to resign myself to peanuts served in newspaper cones as starters, *bhutta* as the main course and Vicks cough drops as dessert, but failed. I snapped at him when he offered me a *narial pani* and coldly said that I'd actually prefer drinking it in a more refined atmosphere, where it's delicately referred to as tender coconut water. He looked surprised and said he didn't think I was that kind of girl. Since the phrase 'that kind of girl' usually refers to women whose telephone numbers are scribbled on loo walls, my hackles rose, but he hastily explained that he was referring to those champagne-is-mother's-milk-to-me wannabe socialites. He was right, I had to grudgingly admit. I'm definitely not that kind of girl. I'm more the dhaba, pass-the-pickled-onions type. I only wish it wasn't so painfully obvious. I realized then that I badly needed to acquire a little class. I blame my sodding parents for that. They could have sent me to a finishing school in Switzerland or genetically gifted me an aquiline nose so I could at least look like I could tell fish and butter knives apart.

We decided to compromise and called for a home delivery on the shoe-polishwallah's cellphone. With a medium pepperoni pizza, French fries and colas on their way to the red jeep after the third palm tree opposite the Oberoi Hotel, I settled down for a very unusual date.

Way past midnight he drove me home, gave me a chaste peck on the cheek and vroomed off. Needless to say, I was sorely disappointed. I still didn't know if his palms were pulpy and sweaty like a frog's or firm and cool. Also, he had me wondering whatever happened to the good old French-kiss-in-return-for-French-fries rule.

I was two minutes late for work the next morning. As I dashed to sign the muster, the creepy Anglo-Indian receptionist yanked it away from me and thrust the late muster under my nose. I didn't want to beg and plead (hell, why give the attention-hungry bitch that satisfaction?) so I grimly signed it with a cutting remark. 'Mavis darling, I think you forgot to shave this morning. Your Hitler moustache is bristling with importance.'

I realized New Guy was behind me only when I heard him chuckle. I gave him a broad wink as Mavis choked indignantly over my jibe and sailed in. He bounded after me like a playful puppy and parked himself on my desk. We had a pleasant time shooting the breeze, despite the fact that I kept looking over my shoulder involuntarily, just in case Tenaz arrived and stabbed me with a Swiss army knife. I was in a good mood. Things were even better the rest of the day, when I found zillions of soppy mails from Software in my inbox. I replied with trenchant Dorothy Parker-ish wit and was oh-so-pleased with the way things were going. Thanks to him, I hadn't thought of Low Life for at least seven hours at a stretch. But, you know, what they say is true: never be so happy that you think life is perfect because, before you know it, you're ignominiously tripped up.

My ego was toppled disastrously that evening by Software himself. We weren't supposed to meet that day because there was this mega office dinner party to celebrate our escalating billings. 'Kow-tow to clients, lick ass if need be, play walkie-talkie toilet paper,' was the veiled instruction in the office memo and I'd gone back to the hostel to change into something decent. I was surprised when I saw Software's car parked outside and, admittedly, a little flattered. I foolishly thought he was so driven with longing that he'd decided to snatch a few minutes with me.

He grinned lopsidedly when he saw me arrive and thrust a bouquet of roses into my hands. As I grasped it, his expression became sombre. I honestly thought he was going to tell me he'd just discovered that his pet goldfish had gill cancer or something. He abruptly broke into my second-guessing. 'Erm, have you ever wondered why I've never made moves on you?'

I vehemently denied it. I couldn't let on that I'd spent the past few nights wondering about his lack of sex drive. After all, most guys have to be handcuffed by the end of the first date. Monica had kind of drilled it into me that he may be gloriously gay or bisexual. Jo was supposed to check with Lust Bug and revert. We were still waiting for the news on which way he swung. 'Well, um, the thing is, hell, I just have to tell you before I lose courage,' he said, looking really nervous.

'What, you slather on your mum's lipstick and eyeshadow when she's at a kitty party?' I don't know how that slipped out, but it did and I almost kicked myself. I really have a chronic case of foot-in-mouth disease, which probably explains why I never make it to the top 10,000 of popularity charts.

He looked indignant at that. 'No way!' Then he shifted

his gaze to his feet. They were enormously large, I noticed with horror; he probably left Yeti-sized footprints in his wake. 'Um, the thing is, my ex-girlfriend is back from the States and she, um, wants to get back and um . . .'

I'd heard enough and abruptly cut him short. 'Hey, that's fabulous!' I gushed like a waterfall in full spate during a good monsoon year. 'Congrats, go back with open arms.'

He was gobsmacked. I couldn't have achieved better results if I'd hit him on the head with a blunt object.

'No! It's not that easy. I really like you, don't want to stop seeing you. I'm still not sure, maybe you and I . . .'

I cut him short again, coldly this time. 'Hello, don't bother to toss a coin because my mind is made up.'

He persisted. 'Look, I thought we really hit it off well together. Can we be friends at least?'

'Sure,' I said generously, 'but don't call me. I'll call you. And hey, thanks for these.' I held up the bouquet and dashed into the hostel. I heard him call my name, but I didn't look back. My eyes were beginning to fill up with wimpish tears, and the last thing I wanted was to look like a soppy loser in public again.

I junked the flowers in the first waste-paper basket I saw. Going by my cheap dates with him, he'd probably stolen them from a graveyard. I looked longingly at the cough syrup when I entered the room but desisted. I couldn't go to the office bash drugged out of my skull.

God knows what I'd say to the goddamn clients. I couldn't avoid the do either, much as I wanted to, because Super-Bitch Boss would give me minus marks in my appraisals under Client-Interaction Skills. I tried to console myself with the fact that for a change, I was the other woman, not the sinned-against true love. Even that failed. Hell, I was just a total loser. I collapsed on the bed and let waves of self-pity wash over me. When I'd finally purged myself, I realized that I was sodding late and got dressed super-quick—just like a man. Emotional trauma clearly induces hormone-altering effects.

The first thing I did when I entered was to suck up to clients. I was so depressed, I'd even lost my sense of humour. I was as deathly boring as the tight-assed sods, which I think they appreciated. I even overheard one tell the other that I was the only sensible person they'd met in advertising. Not a compliment coming from them; it made me feel totally brain-dead. Once I'd scratched every important person off my duty list, I hit the bar with a vengeance and hung around alone in a dark corner of the lawn. I saw New Guy in a tight clinch with Tenaz on the dance floor. Unfortunately, our eyes met and a few minutes later, he pulled her towards me. 'Why are you playing solitaire?' he cheerfully asked.

Because no guy will ever give me one, is what I wanted to say, but I just shrugged and took a deeper swig. A creepy, sloshed-way-over-the-limit servicing trainee staggered up to us. 'Lesh dansh,' he said, grabbing my hand. I shook the cretin off. He grabbed Tenaz's hand next and dragged her, screaming and kicking, to the dance floor. Just then, from the corner of my eye, I saw Super-Bitch Boss slinking off into the shadows with a very, very senior chap from the agency.

I let out a snort of contempt and raised my glass at them. 'There she goes, working hard towards her next promotion.'

New Guy laughed. 'You really despise her, huh?'

I shook my head. 'Yes. Actually, no. Not her. She's just fighting the glass ceiling in her own stupid, misguided way. No, the thing is, I really despise men. They'll sleep with anything that comes their way. It's true, I guess, what they say about public-school boys, they'll even make out with goats.'

New Guy protested. 'Hey, I was in boarding school, I never ever made out with a goat.' And then he did something really surprising. He swung me around to face him, looked me deep in the eye and said, 'In fact, the only protein-based life form I want to sleep with right now is you.'

I was stunned. Even Low Life hadn't been as direct in his desire to see me stripped down to my undies. But I always recover fast. 'Yeah? Do you have protection?'

Without shifting his gaze, New Guy whipped out his wallet and brandished a strip of condoms.

'Nah, wrong brand,' I swiftly said. I looked unruffled when I said that. My voice didn't even waver. But I was shaking inside. This guy was way out of my league. Low Life was cool too, but he was conventional cool, if you know what I mean. He wore flat fronts when flat fronts were in, he even wooed women according to the ancient rule book, where 'I love you' is an accepted euphemism for 'Take off your panties.' New Guy, on the other hand, called a spade a spade. Refreshing, but unnerving.

Anyway, he shrugged and scrunched up his eyes at me. I couldn't help noticing that he looked devastatingly sexy when he did that. 'That's the problem with women. They're only into teasing.'

My rejoinder was swift. 'And you know the problem with men? They're only into cheating. That's why,' I said, giving him my most superior look, 'I prefer Hershey's Kisses to any slimy man's.'

Saying thus, I sailed away to replenish my drink.

nine

Funny, but after being dumped unceremoniously by Low Life and perfunctorily by Software, I stopped having Monday-morning blues. I used to get Friday-evening blues instead, when practically everyone in the hostel (except Twisted Spinster Warden, her parrot, a Madeleine Albright clone, a Rabri Devi clone and me) dressed up to the nines and hit the bright lights. The humiliation was unbearable and I was delighted to be back at work the following Monday, relieved that I had something to do. I entered office bright and early (even before the creepy receptionist), and discovered a pack of Hershey's Kisses on my desk. I stared at it, puzzled, for a few seconds. Then it dawned on me. New Guy really was something else. I assumed he was in office too, but decided to collect myself before I thanked him. I had to watch out for this guy. I had to stop myself from succumbing to his quirky charms or it would only be a matter of time before I started unconsciously doodling his name on my writing pad under Tenaz's watchful glare. I called Jo for advice and whispered, 'Any idea where I can get a chastity belt?'

Jo was excited. Women who are happily engaged or married really want their best friends to be happily engaged or married too. That way they have someone, apart from their mums, to compare teflon-coated frying pans and detergent powders with, without feeling like frumps. I told her categorically that he was already taken or at least booked by Tenaz. She scoffed. 'Till your Tenaz has a diamond sparkling on her finger, he's free for all. Go for it. I like his spunky sense of humour.'

I didn't agree. You don't poach on other people's game. It's not done, no matter how badly you want it. And thank god I'd decided not to pile on to him, because a few minutes later, Tenaz waltzed into our cubicle humming a schmaltzy song. I think it was Wet Wet Wet's *Love is all around me,* you know, the one that goes, 'I feel it in my fingers, I feel it in my toes, something something . . .' She looked as pleased as Punch too, and when I raised an inquiring eyebrow at her, she positively gushed. 'My plan's working. New Guy really more than likes me.'

I bit back my disappointment and tried to look happy for her. 'How d'you know?' I asked, curious.

'Oh, just things he said to me yesterday. He was over for lunch,' she said airily and went back to her humming.

It was beginning to irritate me. I mean, singing or humming is just not her thing. I didn't really want to know what New Guy said to her, but I had to get her to talk to stop that insane tuneless humming. 'So *what* did he say?'

'Well, we had this really heavy chat and, you know, I was discussing ex-boyfriends and things just to suss him out and told him that I'd been in love once. Then I asked him if he'd ever been in love. He said, not love but lust, too many times to count. And I asked him if he was in lust with anyone at the moment and he just sort of shrugged and said, maybe.' She looked triumphant.

'Maybe he wasn't talking about you,' I said tartly.

'Oh, he most certainly was!'

'How do you know?'

'What do you mean how do I know? One just knows these things.' Tenaz looked a bit pissed off, so I stopped my version of the Spanish Inquisition. Anyway, my plan had obviously succeeded, because she stopped humming and smiling vacantly into space. I'd given her something to think about.

I'd given myself something to think about too. New Guy had to be given a very wide berth. He was clearly into two-timing, like all the other men I'd known. Fortunately, I forgot about him soon enough. I didn't even have time to thank him for the Hershey's Kisses, Super-Bitch Boss saw to that. She was in a foul mood. She'd probably overheard someone discussing her wanton ways at the party. Hey, the office was buzzing with the sleazy news, and she wanted to verbally thrash us into frightened submission. She bombed everything that came her way and sent us back to the drawing board with sundry fleas in our ears. Just when I was contemplating becoming a suicide bomber in her cabin (the only worthwhile cause to die for, in my opinion), I got a phone call from the headhunter I'd spoken to. She'd fixed up a meeting for me at 9 p.m. that night. I was relieved to learn that it was at the Bombay Gym bar—I really needed a couple of stiff ones to unwind. That piece of news kept me going as I churned out reams of copy with my fingers crossed, not a very easy feat, but one I'd perfected since I became Super-Bitch Boss's favourite whipping boy.

The bitch kept us in late, religiously consigning every word I'd written to the paper shredder. Just when I thought I was going to have to cancel my meeting, she picked up her bag and swept out of the office. Tenaz was at the water cooler at that time and reported that the very same very, very senior person Super-Bitch Boss had obviously traded DNA smears with at the party left in the same elevator. The gossip mills began churning again, but I didn't wait to hear what they were saying. It was 8.45 p.m. and I'd already decided that if I didn't get that job, I'd buy a one-way ticket to New York and hurl myself off the Empire State Building. I dashed out and was hurtling down the stairs, because our office building had the slowest lifts in the world (turtles are zippier) when I heard hurried footsteps behind me and my name being hollered. It was a breathless New Guy, wanting to know if I'd like to join Tenaz and him for an old movie that night, *Annie Hall*. Wow, I thought, he liked Woody Allen too! Now I had one more reason to watch out for him or else I'd be putty in his hands.

'No thanks,' I replied, equally breathless, 'I've seen it at least six times. Enjoy.' On the way to the Bombay Gym, I made up a nonsensical poem in my head: 'Tenaz's property's not that hot/ I will poach him not.' I *had* to say it to myself over and over again, because I was sorely tempted to toss him over my shoulder and drag him into my cave. Not for sex, well, not just sex, but conversation too. He was bloody interesting.

I kind of liked my new potential Creative Director. He was already on his seventh Johnnie Walker on the rocks when I arrived, and full of bonhomie. He made me feel really comfortable, like an equal almost. Before the first fifteen minutes were up, the job was mine. I suspect I got it, not because of my pathetically slim portfolio, but on the strength of my awesome talent for drinking. I'd knocked back two extra large rums in a very short while, a good indicator that I was made of sterling stuff. After we'd discussed the filthy-lucre part, we leaned back like a couple of seasoned barflies and discussed the lighting in an arty Satyajit Ray flick neither of us had seen but had just read reviews of. We bonded like true pseudo-intellectuals. This made me feel even more secure, a sensation I really enjoy. It was like being back at my college canteen in Calcutta. My appointment letter, I was told, would be ready the next day.

We reluctantly staggered out after the bar closed and before I got back to the hostel I called Dad to tell him that he could stop sending me pin money, I would be earning much, much more. Admittedly not enough to bathe in pink champagne daily, but more than sufficient for a weekly hair-rinse with beer. Dad was horrified. He didn't think I should quit. He's very old-fashioned, my dad, the sort who believes that the only time you leave your first job is either when you get a gold-plated wristwatch and a slim pension or when you're carried out on a stretcher to the morgue. Whichever comes first. I had to waste good money calming him down, telling him that in advertising it's different; if you don't change your job as often as you change your undies people think you're a write-off.

I spent the rest of the night gloating over my new job and writing drafts of my resignation letter. I made sure to get in as many puns as I could, just to spite Super-Bitch Boss. My favourite one was:

Dear Super-Bitch Boss,
You're barking up the wrong tree if you think I'll roll over and play dead for you all my life. I'm off to pastures new.

P.S. I have several bones to pick with you.

Monica, however, forced me to change that to a saccharine-sweet, 'This is to inform you, blah blah, it's breaking my heart, blah blah, would love to work with you again, blah blah' grovelling sort of letter. She firmly said I shouldn't burn my bridges. For a change, Jo agreed with her. So I gave in, albeit reluctantly. I just couldn't wait to nonchalantly toss my resignation letter at the bitch the next morning. She deserved it after the tepid appraisal she'd given me. The best part was I had loads of leave left. I only had to lick her shoes for another couple of weeks. I'd decided not to tell anyone I was quitting until Super-Bitch Boss signed my release papers. She had a reputation for creating a stink if she ever found out she was the last to know and became exceedingly difficult, almost like a government of India official. You know, the ones that keep you waiting in a queue while they scratch their elbows and take frequent tea breaks and, when you finally get to them, tell you (triumphantly) that you've got the wrong window.

When I entered office the next morning, I heard peals of laughter emanating from New Guy's cabin. I stepped in, curious, to find him ribbing Tenaz.

'Hey, did you guys enjoy the movie?' I asked.

Tenaz grimaced and gave it a thumbs-down. 'Depressing.'

New Guy shook his head at her like she'd had a

lobotomy or something. 'Just because it didn't have an and-they-lived-happily-ever-after ending, she hated it. You women only appreciate chick-flicks.'

I rushed to defend my sex. Not purely out of altruistic motives, I really love a good, old-fashioned romantic movie as much as the next bimbette. I strained my brain to recall a chick-flick that wasn't vapid. I had a feeling he'd sneer at my favourite, gut-achingly funny romantic comedy, *When Harry Met Sally*, too. Then, inspiration struck. 'Hey, not all chick-flicks have happy endings, what about *Romeo and Juliet?*'

New Guy scoffed at that. 'I'll tell you one thing about Romeo and Juliet. If they'd been married to each other long enough, they'd have killed each other instead of themselves.'

'God, that's so cynical!' Tenaz moaned. She looked really upset.

But I was laughing hysterically. From what I'd seen of life, he was so damn right. 'I don't know Tenaz, I'm beginning to buy it.'

After I stopped shaking with laughter, I noticed that he'd kind of decorated his room with bits of his personality. About a zillion Garfield strips were pinned on his soft board. He even had a Garfield mug on his desk. That said a lot about him, lots of appealing things, and I felt my interest in him flicker briefly again. I quickly quelled it. 'Hey, you're quite a Garfield freak, huh?'

'Hmmm . . . Greatest philosopher in the world. I think he gives Hegel and Nietzsche a good run for their money. And I can't stand Kant.'

I grinned in appreciation of his pun, but Tenaz was looking totally at sea. She valiantly attempted to swing the conversation in her favour again, and deliberately turned to face him. God, women in love will kill even their best friends if they think their boyfriends like them. 'So lunch at my place Sunday, then?'

Instead of replying, New Guy looked pointedly at me. 'You coming?'

I could tell that the invitation didn't include me, so I shrugged in a vague way.

Tenaz was signalling wildly to me and mouthing, 'Say no.' I shrugged again and Tenaz rushed to rescue herself. 'She can't come. She has a hot date.'

I nodded and walked out. My presence in the room was evidently giving Tenaz high blood pressure. I realized that if I didn't leave soon, her varicose veins would probably burst—not a pretty sight.

'Yeah, really hot. I call him Scorchy,' was my parting shot. For the next hour or so, a voice in my head was sternly admonishing me, 'Repeat after me: Tenaz's property's not that hot/I will poach him not.'

The minute Super-Bitch Boss sailed into office, I shot into her cabin and wordlessly shoved my polite, 'So long and thanks for all the crap' letter into her clawed paws.

She looked stricken after she read it, like I'd just bitten the hand that fed me. 'You can't go,' she shrieked.

'Why not?' I was firm.

'Because I trained you, for god's sake! I invested so much time and effort to turn you into the half-baked writer you are today.'

I eyed her coldly and unsheathed my claws for a change. The bitch had begged for it. 'Yeah, that's precisely why I'm leaving. I need a more talented baker to complete the job.'

I didn't tell Monica about that part of the conversation. She'd have laid on that 'I told you not to burn bridges' bullshit real thick, a philosophy I just don't buy. Hey, if I've decided not to walk down a certain path again, what does it matter to me if the bridge is charred beyond recognition? This corporate, let's-pretend-we-love-each-other-while-we-simultaneously-stick-pins-into-voodoo-dolls-of-each-other crap is only for cretins. I'd rather die a miserable loser than a creepy, materialistic slimeball. 'Poor but honest' is my mantra.

ten

I have just one word to describe the next matrimonial guy Mum set me up with: yuck. He was an archetypal gym jock, the guy in the extra-tight lycra tee you see flexing his biceps, triceps and goddamn quadraceps or whatever they are at the gym, facing the mirror, of course. Hell, I'd much rather have had dinner with King Kong, his IQ level would probably have been higher. This one had been brought up in dumb *Duh*li, a city where the average Joe thinks that the 'mc' in Einstein's e=mc^2 theory stands for *maader chod* (Hindi for 'motherfucker'). The jerk was chauvinistic enough to order for both of us, he didn't even wait for me to consult the menu card. When he discovered that even the crummy restaurant he took me to was too upmarket to serve his favourite North Indian veggie meal, *rajma-chawal*, he ordered salad. The only woman I can think of who'd enjoy his choice of cuisine is Jessica Rabbit. I rated him a minus-ten on ten when he proudly informed me that he hired the same personal trainer as Bollywood muscle-boy Salman Khan. And then he did the unforgivable: he grabbed my upper arm, squeezed it hard and informed me that it was flabby. My abs could do with some desperate toning too, he added helpfully.

I didn't even offer to split the bill (why should I have, the food was shit). But I did inform him that his brains needed a bit of a workout. 'Try jigsaw puzzles if you can't read,' was my farewell line, 'some of the pictures are quite pretty.' Mum was clearly getting desperate. The signs were all there. This was not the sort of guy she'd even consider for herself. A man who preferred cottage cheese to tandoori chicken? Come on, what sort of libido would he have? Mum was, after all, a woman of the world.

Now that I knew I was leaving the agency in a few days, it was difficult to concentrate on work. I'd also become very lax, sailing in late and leaving early. Super-Bitch Boss tried to haul me up for that, but I outstared her. She averted her eyes, proving my pet theory that all bullies are cowards. That's why I just can't bring myself to respect them. Tenaz had been acting mighty strange of late, and New Guy seemed too preoccupied to even smile at me. I mean, they'd stopped asking me to join them for a coffee or a beer in the evenings, and I'd gotten quite used to that. While I was wary of New Guy, I'd really enjoyed chilling out with him. We had the same favourite authors, he had this amazing repertoire of stories about his life at IIM where he was the celebrated unofficial porn writer on campus, his irrepressible humour made me laugh even more than Woody Allen and Alan Coren combined did, and hey, he was an engineering grad too, he also knew his music. I mean, he even understood what I meant when I'd said that of all the Dire Straits albums I'd heard, *Love Over Gold* was the most soul-stirring. And he was certain Robert Palmer's voice was so perfect because his pants were ridiculously tight. But most important, he turned me on because he was so full of life—unlike me. If I placed both of us in A.A. Milne's Pooh series, I would be Eeyore, the hopelessly pessimistic donkey, and New Guy would be Tigger, brimming over with enthusiasm and boundless energy. Jo had joined us for a drink once and she'd quite liked him too, after their 'bosom' argument was resolved. Well, he said it was 'bosom' and she insisted it could be 'bosoms' too, and they hated each other violently till I rushed to a nearby bookshop and consulted a dictionary because I wasn't sure myself. Fortunately, it turned out that both of them were right, so they clinked beer mugs and made up. Tenaz, of course, was totally out of it again. I just can't understand people who aren't fascinated by words. They miss out on so much.

At first, I thought Tenaz and New Guy were giving me a wide berth because they'd found out from the grapevine that I was leaving and they were upset that they weren't the first to know. Later, I realized that it went far deeper than that. On my second-last day at work, the day Tenaz should have offered to buy me a farewell lunch, after all I had been her copy partner for years, she was incredibly rude. I decided to ignore it and asked her out to lunch instead. She refused. Baffled, I asked her what the matter was, but she glared at me and said, 'Don't tell me you don't know already.' I didn't, but I shut up. Maybe she had PMT or some other hormonal screw-up, I thought. Stuff like that is excusable. A few seconds later, New Guy arrived at our cubicle, ignored my cheerful grin and asked Tenaz out for lunch. She accepted. As I watched them leave, chattering happily, I was certain that the world was celebrating International Treat-Arti-Like-a-Leper Day.

Later that evening, I caught New Guy in the studio doing a throaty impersonation of the lead-in music to Deep Purple's *Smoke on the water*. He did it real well. My heart kind of lurched, I mean, this is the sort of thing that *really* turns me on. It's such a delightfully insane thing to do. Our eyes met and I grinned at him and was about to gush all over him in true groupie fashion, but he gave me a blank stare in response. I shrugged and got back to what I was doing, but it hurt. Much, much more than a cholera shot with a rusted needle.

That night, I had another meet-the-matrimonial-ad-cretin date. Mum was really laying them on thick and fast now. She was clearly worried that the more financially stable I became, the less I'd be interested in marriage.

This guy told me he'd be wearing a Charlie Brown tie and as I scanned the room for the clown, I saw New Guy at a table with a bunch of people I'd never seen before. My heart began to beat faster and I realized with a sinking feeling that I'd probably never see him again after I left that office, and that I'd miss him. God Almighty, I was in love! I'd been looking for love in the strangest places, just like in that Uriah Heep song, *July morning*. And all along, he'd been there and I hadn't really thought he was *the one*, apart from mild lusting. I mean, mentally, he really turned me on. He was funny, intelligent, even more irreverent than I was, and, what do you know, maddeningly sexy too, if you scrunched up your eyes and looked at him from a certain angle. But, to be honest, even if he'd looked like Gaston Leroux's physically-challenged phantom of the opera, I'd have grabbed him. Looks aren't important to me; mental stimulation is. I wished I'd listened to Jo and snatched him out of Tenaz's limpet-like grasp. And I wished that even if it were a case of unrequited love, we could have been friends. I couldn't bear the idea of not even talking to him any more, he interested me *that* much. His quirky take on life left me breathless. I forced myself to drag my gaze away from him and found Mr Charlie Brown-Tie.

The meal passed in a blur. I drank way too much and barely spoke. Mr Charlie Brown-Tie looked appalled and informed me in a concerned way that I had a drinking problem.

'Alcoholism runs in my family,' I blithely slurred. I wasn't lying, exactly. My cousin had once passed out at the age of seven after knocking back a full bottle of Bailey's Irish Cream in one afternoon while her mum was napping. 'It was better than Mars bars,' was all she staunchly said in her defence, after her hangover had subsided. Well, that statement effectively knocked out Mr Charlie Brown-Tie as a contender for my hand. Not that I cared. He was just a measly two on ten. He had awful ferret-like teeth and annoying puritanical values. When I got back to the hostel, I listened to *July morning*, drained a full bottle of cough syrup and wept. For New Guy, not Low Life. Strange, but true. Time had finally done its number, but I still wasn't happy.

My farewell tea party at the office the next day was pleasant, though. Despite the fact that both Tenaz and New Guy were conspicuous by their absence. After the mandatory *samosas*, chips and colas had done the rounds, I was asked to make a speech. I gamely stood on a chair and said, 'I've had very many happy moments here, but this is my happiest.' Super-Bitch Boss looked like she'd bitten into a very sour plum and left the room, slamming the door real hard. *Fuck her*, I thought, *and fuck Tenaz and New Guy too, I'd survive*.

I was given a copy of the *Kamasutra* as a farewell

present. 'Thanks guys,' I said, holding it up for all to see, 'but the only use I'll have for this is to prop up my hostel chair's shaky leg.'

Darius offered to execute a few moves with me if I paid him good money. Great, I thought to myself, now it's common knowledge that I'm such a loser, I'll have to pay for sex. But still, I was in a fairly decent mood. After all, I'd never have to suffer Super-Bitch Boss again.

It was only 4.30 p.m., when my farewell party wound up and I still had a few hours to kill before I saw the last of that lot. I decided to say individual farewells to the handful of people I'd really liked. I passed New Guy's cabin several times and finally mustered up enough courage to say goodbye to him. The truth is I really wanted to be with him one last time. I knocked tentatively at his door and almost shot off when he looked up. He didn't exactly seem happy to see me, but something kept me rooted to the spot. 'Um, I just wanted to say bye.'

'Oh yes, you're leaving. Come in,' he said shortly. I continued to linger at the door and he asked me to sit down. 'Relax, I'm too tired to molest you. Besides, the door's open,' he said dryly.

The only intelligent answer I could come up with to this extremely strange statement was: 'Huh?' I sat down anyway, and told him I'd forgotten to thank him for the Hershey's Kisses.

He grinned at that (I *told* you, he's irrepressible) and asked if I'd enjoyed them.

That's when Mum's genes kicked in again. I boldly looked him in the eye and said, 'Yup, I did. But, you know, I've discovered that I prefer the real thing.'

New Guy nodded, looking a trifle disinterested. 'I gathered. Tenaz tells me you're practically engaged to a very, erm, how did she put it, hot guy.'

My hackles rose. And when I get angry I can make ten-armed goddesses who slay demons by exercising supernatural powers seem like wishy-washy wimps. I don't explode. I just get incredibly sub-zero and freeze my enemies. Those are my dad's genes. When he's really pissed off, he's like an iceberg down your back. My voice had a steely edge to it as I said, 'Really? So how come I still take cold showers?'

New Guy leaned forward. He looked interested. Very, very interested. 'Are you telling me you're not seeing anyone?'

'Yes.'

'Are you telling me that you did *not* tell Tenaz that I should lay off you, that I was coming on too strong?'

'Yes.' My voice had become colder.

'Are you telling me that Tenaz was lying?'

'*Fucking* yes.'

'And,' his voice softened, 'are you telling me that you're interested in me?'

'Yes, yes, oh, yes!' I said that so hysterically, I sounded like I needed to be straitjacketed and confined to a padded cell or something.

'So,' he said, with a gleam in his eye, 'how would you rate me on the "hot" scale?'

'Well,' I considered, 'I would probably turn into molten volcanic lava if you touched me right now.'

'Give me a live demo,' he dared, coming closer. And then he shut the door and pulled me towards him.

'Um, the door is made of glass,' I reminded him, 'and Tenaz is outside, looking in.'

'Fuck Tenaz,' he said.

'No, fuck me instead,' I urged.

'Your place or mine?' was the rejoinder.

We left the office immediately after. During an incredibly romantic dinner (hey, we didn't even need candlelight and champagne to get the pheromones flowing) I asked him why he spent so much time at Tenaz's place if it was me he'd always wanted. He told me that it was for two reasons: one, he hoped I'd be there too, seeing that Tenaz and I were good friends. And two, her mum's *dhansak* really turned him on. His dad was a Parsee and after he walked out on the family, New Guy's Keralite mum stopped cooking Parsee food altogether. She also got rid of the framed pictures of Zarathustra, the tacky coronation plates, the fussy antimacassars and the ancient Morris Minor. There wasn't even a hint of anything Parsee left in the house apart from her children. Them she fought a bitter battle to keep. New Guy swore that the next time he got an uncontrollable urge for *dhansak*, he'd pig out at one of those tiny, homely restaurants scattered around the Fort area that served almost-as-good-as-home Parsee fare. When he finally drove me back to the hostel, we passed the chemist's. I waved at the owner, Mr Shah, and thought, *I don't know if this thing with New Guy will work out. Nothing ever does for me. And if it doesn't, I hope the sodding government hasn't banned cough syrups by the time I'm dumped again.*

eleven

Okay, so I got a new job. I got over Low Life. I even got New Guy as a bonus. The sun was shining, the birdies were singing, god was in his heaven, all was right with the world and guess what happened? I discovered that I was frigid. I suppose it was god's way of reminding me that I was toe jam in his eyes.

It just wasn't fair. I had a few days to kill till I started work at the new place and New Guy had taken a few days off to, as he put it in his wickedly laid-back way, get to know me better. The venue was a beach resort, a little away from the city. It was Gorai beach where you swim not with exotic fish but with discarded plastic and foil wrappers. Despite the filth, the ambience was heavenly. Wordsworth would have waxed eloquent. I mean, it was more picturesque than bloody daffodils.

But to get back to my problem. Oh, I was very turned on, I could neck all right. But I couldn't go any further, all thanks to that Bitch Doctor who had got me thinking I was pregnant. I was scared. I didn't ever want to experience that sickening fear again. Initially, New Guy thought I was being coy, and was understanding and all that crap. But finally, on our second day there, his frustration began to show. 'For god's sake, Arti, we're adults!' His voice had an edge to it that made me shiver.

I had to come clean with him, and I stuttered, 'Look, I know. It's just that I, um, can't. Hell, I was almost pregnant once.'

New Guy stared at me in disbelief, like I was crazy or something. 'What do you mean "almost"?' he asked threateningly.

I shrugged. 'Well, it turned out that I wasn't.'

He rubbed the back of his neck and sighed deeply. 'Okay, let's not get carried away here. I'm trying very hard to understand where you're coming from. Granted, condoms are not 100 per cent safe, but you could use an oral contraceptive, huh?'

I really didn't like the tone of his voice. He was talking down to me like I was a congenital idiot. I raised my eyebrows coldly at him as I delivered what I still believe is my best punchline to date: 'Oh, I already am using the world's best oral contraceptive: the word "no".'

New Guy buried his face in his hands. I stared at my toes. We were silent for a really long time. I was thinking that maybe Twisted Spinster Warden had been smart to get a parrot. I mean, the parrot wouldn't dump her for not wanting to put out. Parrots are not demanding creatures by nature. And you can always turn them into a tandoori snack if they annoy you. New Guy broke into my reverie, surprised me with an affectionate hug and said, 'You sure it's not because I don't turn you on?'

I said a muffled 'yes'.

'Okay. Then let's get you sorted out fast, because this abstinence is killing me.' He buttoned up his shirt and held out his hand. 'Let's go for a drive. I want you to meet someone special.' He refused to tell me where he was taking me and the car wove its way back into the city. He finally slowed down at a picturesque sea-facing bungalow in Juhu that bore the sign: Dr Parikh, Psychiatrist.

'Nice chap,' New Guy said chattily, as he switched off the engine. 'I spent a lot of time with him after my parents got divorced.'

My jaw dropped. I couldn't believe he'd taken me to a shrink. 'What, you think I need therapy because I won't put out?'

He shrugged and coolly said, 'Choose. My couch or his.'

Well, I guess he had a point, the point being that if I didn't put out, it was goodbye forever, nice knowing you. This guy was tough. We sat in silence again. And then I put my hand on his and said, 'Any idea where we can get industrial-strength condoms from?' I had decided to fight this mental block on my own.

We were back in our room at the resort with zillions of different brands of condoms scattered on the bed and many floating overhead. We'd bought a truckload of them in all the shapes, sizes, colours and fragrances available, you name it, we had it. Honestly, the chemist we got them from must have thought we were opening a brothel or someplace equally kinky. He fastidiously refused to touch our money in case he got herpes or something, he made his assistant pick it up.

New Guy's job was to blow up the condoms and knot them. Mine was to stab each one with a very sharp pin. I finally found the brand I was looking for, one that refused to burst even after several sharp jabs. I tested every single one in the pack and was relieved that they were all as sturdy as tractor tyres. 'Demo over. Peel off your clothes,' I announced cheerfully. But I was feeling a bit shaky. After all, this was the moment of truth: the next few minutes would decide whether we'd part as friends or score mileage points at weekend resorts.

Sex, I discovered that day, is like swimming or cycling. No matter how long you take a break from it, you never forget the moves. A couple of hours later we were already planning our next getaway, it was just so amazing. What made me feel even better was that my belt buckled up at a previously unused notch.

'Hey, what do you know! *Cosmo* was right. Sex *does* burn up calories.' New Guy solemnly promised that before the next day dawned, he'd make sure I was competition for an Ethiopian beauty queen on a bathroom scale. I took him up on that.

When I returned from the beach resort without a peeling nose or even a light tan, Monica and Jo weren't impressed, just a bit wary. Monica took off first. 'Don't jump into it, Arti. You've already been hurt once. Find out more about him first.'

'I know lots already,' I said sullenly. Honestly, they were worse than my goddamn parents.

'Yeah? Like what?' Monica said, her voice dripping with cynicism.

I rattled off his biography. 'He has a sister in marketing, his mum's a school principal and . . .'

Monica interrupted. 'A principal? Whoa! Stop there! You've always had a problem with authority figures. You just can't stand them. You always deliberately rub them up the wrong way.'

I ignored her and continued. 'His parents divorced when he was little and his mum brought him up.'

'Uh-oh, watch out,' Monica interjected again, 'he'll probably be a commitment phobe.'

Jo agreed whole-heartedly. 'Yup, even sex hold-back or charm school won't work here. You'd better not get into it. Does he play air guitar?'

That floored me. 'What's air guitar got to do with commitment phobia?'

Jo assured me that all men who played air guitar were whimsical Peter Pans by nature and never settled down.

I was advised to avoid them like the plague.

Monica nodded. 'Jo's right. Ten out of ten men who play air guitar never get married.'

I got really annoyed. I mean, I was happy after such a long time and all my best friends wanted to do was rain on my parade. 'Back off, guys. I don't know and don't care if he plays air guitar or not. We haven't been to a rock show yet, dammit. The point is, I've finally discovered that there's life after being dumped. Let me enjoy myself for a bit. Marriage isn't everything.'

I knew that line would get Monica on my side (I can be fairly wily when I choose to) and she rose to the bait. 'Yeah, big deal! Marriage isn't everything.'

Jo looked put off, but remained silent. Those days, I felt really sorry for engaged or married types who hung out with uncommitted singles. We made them feel like they were old-fashioned or something and missing out on loads of fun. What they didn't know was that we secretly envied them, but we never told them that. Why give them the satisfaction? After all, they had so much already. Anyway, I deftly changed the subject by asking Jo what I should wear for my first day at work. She loves girlie stuff like that and she threw herself into the role of wardrobe assistant with great enthusiasm.

I instinctively liked my new place of work. The people were friendly, the atmosphere was cheerful and I had already bonded with the Creative Director. He really was a decent sort, with very high spirits indeed. Whenever they started sinking, he'd have another Scotch-on-the-rocks transfusion. The man had a well-stocked bar in his cabin. He'd get the mixers and ice cubes from the pantry. Also, he was pretty generous with his expense account in the after-hours. A far cry from stingy-mingy Super-Bitch Boss, who'd take us out for lunch and then claim she'd forgotten her cash and card at home. The only problem I had with him was that he'd become a crashing bore when he was smashed and tell us sickly stuff like he was so talented because he looked at the world through the eyes of a child and crap. And sometimes he'd recount his childhood memories like the time his dad put him on his shoulders so he could get an unhindered view of the Ram Leela and all that touchy-feely shit. As if we cared. But apart from that, I could see myself with a very bright career and cirrhosis of the liver in that organization. Within the first week, I'd bought liver tabs, just in case. Mr Shah, the chemist, was astonished that I didn't want cough syrup too. He wanted to know if I was sick. I assured him that I was better than I'd been in months. I honestly did feel better, and the icing on the cake was that my first campaign for a lollipop had been approved in-house and presented (without me) to the client. I was waiting for client feedback.

My cup of joy was still brimming over. New Guy and

I were in the throes of love. It was early days yet, that's when everything is perfect beyond belief, like fiction. He'd just driven me back to the hostel after dinner. As his car sped off, this figure slunk out of the shadows and loomed over me. It was Low Life. He looked grim.

'And just who was that?' he practically spat out.

'Fuck you. It's none of your goddamn business,' I hissed.

He glared at me. I glared back. What gave the cretin the right to ask who I was seeing, considering that he'd ruthlessly booted me out of his life? I turned to go in, but he grabbed my hand and groaned theatrically. 'I miss you real bad.'

'I don't.'

'Look, I made a mistake. I want you back.'

I was aching to ask him if his Bimbo Dogess had dumped him, but I decided to play it real cool instead. 'I don't.'

He became emotional suddenly. 'I'm nothing without you.' His voice broke. 'You were my good luck charm.'

I snatched back my hand from his tight grasp. 'If you want luck, scour the Mahalaxmi racecourse for a horseshoe and take that for a ride instead. I'm through with your shit.'

In the early days after Low Life had dumped me, I used to fantasize about bumping into him after I was happily engaged to a really hot guy. He'd beg me to take

him back and I'd show him the finger. Not the
engagement finger, the other one. Well, at least half that
fantasy came true that night. I wasn't engaged, but at
least I wasn't single. That would have made me a pitiable
figure in his eyes. I couldn't resist sneaking a peek from
the balcony when I went back to my room. He was still
there, standing under a street light, moodily kicking a
stone. And, get this, I noticed a bald patch right on the
top of his head! It made me feel real good. I felt like
whooping with joy and singing Carly Simon's *You're so
vain* at the top of my lungs, but I desisted. After all, I was
well brought up, the nuns had kind of drilled it into our
skulls that we should never laugh at our enemies, not
even when they made asses of themselves. I slept
incredibly well that night, despite the fact that there was
a strong breeze and the decaying stench of Bombay Duck
lingered heavily in the air.

twelve

 It was a blessing that I'd had a good night's sleep, because the next day was an unmitigated disaster. Both professionally and personally.

I'd entered the office with a spring in my step and the same Carly Simon song on my lips. The song died out abruptly when the servicing flunk informed me that my 'Lollipop' campaign had been brutally nuked. The client had dismissed it as too esoteric. My blood pressure rose. The woman was clearly a hardened philistine. I was instructed by the Creative Director to present it all over again. 'Fight it out with her yourself since it's your baby,' he said encouragingly, as he took a large, comforting swig of his Scotch.

Charged, I stormed into the client's office. I could swear I heard the strains of *We shall overcome*, the favourite anthem of Calcutta University's student political parties, pounding in my ears. Only, their heavily-accented version was *Bhe shall obhercaam.* I remember them singing it lustily in our college canteen when the Indian government's liberalization policies allowed Coca-Cola to return to India and our canteen manager started stocking it, hey, it gave him higher profit margins than tea. '*Opposhonskriti*,' the student cadres cried, outraged, 'totally against our culture! Coca-Cola is an imperialist imposition and its sales here will help the American dogs become richer and that money will be used to arm their favourite ally, Pakistan.' Needless to say, our canteen manager returned his crates to the distributor forthwith, *that's* how powerful that anthem is. It didn't work for me, however. Even if I'd sung it out loud, it wouldn't have had any effect. Bombayites value money over principles.

The client was an *avtar* of Frankenstein's monster. Oh, she was hot in the looks department, but she had a cold, cold heart—you know, the sort who'd blithely press the nuclear button to annihilate her competition even if she knew her ailing mother was in the target zone. What do you say to a woman who wants to advertise a fun confectionery product as clinically as a laxative or suppositories, who believes that if advertising people want to get creative they should write sonnets or paint landscapes? I could think of lots of unprintable things to say to her, but I had to bite my tongue because this was an important multinational client. Those sickly-sweet lollipops of hers were the rage all over the globe. What was more relevant, her billings paid my salary and took care of my enjoyable little perks.

I returned to the office with a battered, tattered ego and a new campaign to crack. The first thing I did was to call New Guy. I needed to sound off on Frankenstein's Monster. He laughed uproariously. Encouraged, I added colourful expletives, the sort that are on every seafaring parrot's repertoire. He guffawed even more. Then, still chuckling, he told me that he was taking me to his mum's place for dinner. He said she wanted to see whom he rated higher than Xena, the Warrior–Princess. I'd never met his family before, because New Guy lived on his own in a company flat in the suburbs. I was very curious, yet mildly apprehensive.

Not bad, I thought to myself. Dinner with the family is not something commitment phobes encourage. I ruminated deeply over what would be a decent meet-the-family outfit. I dismissed the idea of wearing a sari or any ethnic stuff. It gives an unmistakable I-am-interested-in-being-the-mother-of-your-only-son's-1000-sons vibe. I wanted to play it sub-zero cool.

Monica barged in while I was rifling through my closet. 'High neck, full sleeves, ankle-length, without a slit,' was her recommendation. Since I didn't have time to hop across to a convent to borrow a nun's habit, I settled for corporate-ish-looking gear instead. Monica critically watched me getting dressed to impress. At the same time, she debriefed me on Phase 2 of the Monica & Jo Inquisition. She provocatively said that I might meet my Waterloo in his loo. Startled, I asked her to expand on that.

'Come on, Arti! Any idiot knows that loos reveal a lot about people. Even the brand of toilet paper would be a telling comment on his family's income levels, educational qualifications, psyche, tastes in music and suchlike. Geddit?' She practically ordered me to study the contents of the bathroom cabinet carefully. I was getting heartily sick of their protective shit. I wished she and Jo would just hire a Hercule Poirot type to do the dirty work. Why couldn't they believe that I wasn't scared of getting hurt, not any more? Once bitten, and you learn enough to protect yourself. I'd even kept track of the time it took to get over Low Life. Guy No. 2 would be shorter, I'd promised myself. I was experienced now. Even if I did get hurt again, it would only be a flesh wound. Those days I seriously believed that Cat Stevens was right when he sang, 'The first cut is the deepest.'

The evening was a disaster. Way more traumatic than suffering an earthquake or a cyclone. His mum was stiff competition for Super-Bitch Boss. She was oh-so-terrifyingly-schoolmarmish too. I even felt guilty about wearing lipstick and not wearing starched, snow-white bloomers. And then, disaster struck again. His sister walked in and I almost had a coronary: she was Frankenstein's Monster. I silently mouthed Sita's prayer

('Mother Earth, swallow me NOW') when our eyes met. She looked astonished too. I'm dead certain New Guy had a gleam in his eye when he made the I-think-you've-met-before introductions. The single thought that ran circles in my head all evening was to avenge myself by putting out a *supari* on him.

His mum wasn't the sort who inspired PC. Instead of engaging in an animated chat about the weather, I found myself minding my Ps and Qs. The conversation was as awkward and uncomfortable as the Louis the somethingth antique chair I was gingerly perched on. I was dead certain it would go for £100 million at Sotheby's or Christie's. I wouldn't have been surprised to see the skeleton of a *Tyrannosaurus rex* or a pterodactyl artistically arranged on the coffee table too. No Kathakali masks I noted, but there was a mandatory Kerala brass lamp, the only clue that this was a South Indian household. I guess their home could be described as tastefully furnished if you enjoy living in a museum of European art. Me, I can't stand antiques. They're things that belonged to dead people. They creep me out.

I didn't enjoy the dinner either. I was concentrating so hard on following the elbows-off-the-table rule, in case I was sharply rapped on the knuckles, that I found it difficult to swallow a morsel. Which was a pity, because the dinner smelt fabulous: she'd made a traditional Keralite fish curry and red rice meal and the aromatic spices lingered tantalizingly in the air. I couldn't believe New Guy preferred *dhansak* to this; his Parsi blood was evidently thicker.

After dinner, I guiltily remembered Monica's instructions about the loo recce. I excused myself and obediently trotted off. I noted with a sinking heart an ancient claw-footed bathtub that looked straight out of a Gothic horror film. My spirits rose at the sight of the bathroom cabinet's contents, though. There were lots of hotel-pinched moisturizers (a heart-warming human foible) and scented, smuggled-from-First-World-countries toiletries. I made a note that none of the shampoos had anti-dandruff labels and was relieved that I could spend the evening with them without worrying about a scalp infection. I found nothing to set off warning bells, nothing even remotely off-putting. Apart from the spooky bathtub, everything was so above board I was certain Monica and Jo would go down on their knees and beg me to marry him.

I made noises about leaving early because I couldn't take the stuffy, starchy atmosphere one second longer. I was humming that song by Ugly Kid Joe, *I hate everything about you,* under my breath. I used to think it was just a fun song before but that night I deeply empathized with the lyrics, especially the hating-the-mother-and-sister part. I also wanted to get to Mr Shah before his shutters rolled down. I desperately needed a cough-syrup fix. I was half-heartedly pressed to stay, but insisted I had important work to catch up on. Frankenstein's Monster eagerly asked me if I was going to be burning the midnight oil for her campaign. I archly told her that I had to write a spot of poetry instead. She looked taken aback but New Guy almost fell out of his chair guffawing.

After New Guy shut the front door behind us he enveloped me in a warm koala bear hug that was more homely than his home. He said he was stark raving crazy about me because I was full of spunk. I retorted that I hated him because he had a warped sense of humour and promptly melted into his arms. He reassured me about his family in the elevator and said that they took time to warm up to new people.

I wasn't convinced. 'You know, the next time I meet your mum, she'll probably make me write "I will not date your son ever again" a hundred times. And what's the bet your sister will rape me at work tomorrow?'

With a slow, lazy smile, he replied that evidently he had a lot in common with his sister, because that's what he was going to do to me right then. 'You're spending the night at my place, right?'

'Wrong. I don't have a night-out pass.'

'Oh, damn! Why the hell didn't you get it?'

'I was saving it up for the weekend. I only get three a week, remember? I live on rations.' I really couldn't have spent that night with him. I hadn't marked a night out and Twisted Spinster Warden would have had a legit reason to throw me out of the hostel. I would rather have slept with someone with an infectious terminal disease than give her that satisfaction.

New Guy stopped the car. 'There's something I've been wanting to ask you, Arti.'

My heart stood still. I was willing to bet my new Hide-the-Blemish foundation cream that he was going to pop the question.

'Will you . . .'

'Yes?' My voice was tremulous.

'Will you move in with me?'

I gasped and shot off a knee-jerk reaction. 'No fucking way! You know what your problem is? You just want to have your tart and eat it too.'

He looked at me, really looked at me. I was totally pissed off. He didn't know how important it was for me to be made an honest woman of. I mean, the liftman in his building used to leer at me like I was a high-class slut or something. It was very humiliating.

'Look, this is the furthest I can go in a relationship,' he said with a shrug. And then the car jerked to a start and within seconds we were back at the hostel. Michael Schumacher be damned, this guy was better Formula One material.

'Think about it,' were his last curt words.

There are no prizes for guessing what Monica, Jo and I animatedly discussed that night: the live-in offer. Jo was glad that I'd made that 'You want to have your tart and eat it too' statement. She said I should have been more explicit, like telling him it had to be marriage or nothing.

I looked at her aghast. Did this woman never learn from my mistakes? 'Are you out of your tiny mind? No way am I going to bring up the M-word ever again. When I said that to Low Life he sprinted away so fast, he didn't even need goddamn steroids to break Ben Johnson's record.'

'Okay,' Jo considered, 'suck up to his mum, then. If she really likes you, she may be the one to persuade him to marry you. She's a school teacher, right? Why don't you discuss the Oedipus complex or something with her, you know? Stuff like that will impress her.'

'Hello, Jo, my dim one, discussing the Oedipus complex with a woman whose son you want to marry is *not* a good idea. She'll think I'm accusing her of incest. Besides, she teaches maths, not literature. And what do I say to a woman like that? "If you have one son and I take him away from you, how many will you have left"? Huh? Are you crazy?'

Really, Jo wasn't thinking those days. All she was knowledgeable about was oven gloves, spice racks, scented candles and his and hers bath towels. Jo was unfazed. 'Well, I think this live-in thingie sucks all the same. What's the point of being in a relationship that's going nowhere?' she asked defiantly.

'The truth is, Jo, I'd rather be in a relationship that's going nowhere than be out of one. I need companionship for as long as I can get it. After Low Life left, I was so lonely I'd even have dated the Boston strangler or Bozo the clown till a better guy came along. Hell, anyone but Mum's arranged-marriage wimps.'

Monica rushed to my rescue. 'My sentiments exactly, Arti. Take the live-in offer. It's not such a bad idea at all.'

'Oh yeah?' Jo snapped at her. 'Maybe not for you stud-muffin, but Arti's not as tough as you are. Or have you forgotten how devastated she was after Low Life? She was in pieces.'

'It's about time she grew up then and took life head-on. Stop making her believe in your puerile and-they-lived-happily-ever-after fairy tales.'

'Look, she's not an aggro alpha-type female like you are.'

'Yeah, but she's not a bottom-of-the-barrel omega-type personality either.'

'Will you guys stop referring to me in the third person as if I wasn't there,' I whined piteously. I hated the way they were making me sound, like I was a hopeless wimp or something. But they ignored me and attacked each other again.

'You know, Jo, you're just a conservative asshole. You can't handle the fact that I'm happy in my relationship with a married man. Not every woman craves marriage the way you do.'

Jo's eyes blazed at that. 'Point No. 1: I do not crave marriage. I did not beg for it. It was offered and I accepted because I love the guy. Point No. 2: If Dev had asked you to marry him, you'd have agreed like a shot. You can kid yourself if you want to, but you can't kid me.'

'How dare you!' Monica thundered.

The conversation was getting into deathly dangerous territory and I had to stop them before they spilt blood on my crisp bedsheets. I'd just changed them that morning and my spare set was in the laundry bag. 'Oh shut up,' I hollered. 'Both of you are goddamn judgmental assholes. Get out of my room if you want to have a cheap bar brawl.' Both of them shut up and looked ashamed of themselves.

'And,' I added for good measure, 'I've made my decision. I'll have to say a firm no anyway, because my middle-class, society-fearing parents will kill me if I move in with him.'

'Why don't you just do a short trial period first,' Monica suggested.

'What do you mean?' I asked.

'Don't give up the hostel yet. Tell Twisted Spinster Warden you're shooting an ad film and will be in and out of town for a month. Check it out. If you prefer staying with him, we'll figure out how to handle your folks.'

I was stunned. Now this was a great idea. 'Worth thinking about,' I said enthusiastically.

'Wait a minute, though,' Monica added. 'You have to do a small test first to find out how comfortable you'd really be with him.'

'Yeah? What kind of test?'

'The next time you're at his apartment, put an egg-yolk pack on your face.'

'What!' Jo and I shrieked in unison.

Monica looked nonplussed at our reaction. 'Hey, if the two of you can handle that, you can handle anything,' she explained. 'Remember, living in is not a piece of cake. Regular waxing schedules have to be maintained and morning breath can dampen the most passionate of spirits.'

'But, but, egg? Are you crazy, Monica? The stench will drive him away instead of bringing him closer to me. Jo, talk her out of this shit!' I appealed.

But Jo wasn't any help. She was convulsed with mirth.

thirteen

What's with men? They only want you when you finally stop wanting them. That realization dawned on me the next morning in the dining room. Monica and I were attacking breakfast, when Twisted Spinster Warden waddled across and handed me a package. 'It came for you last evening, dear, with a bouquet of flowers. I kept the flowers since I know you don't like them.'

'What makes you think I don't like flowers?' I frowned. I mean, she couldn't just filch people's stuff without asking.

'I saw you chucking a bouquet into a dustbin a few months ago,' she countered.

Oh, right. Software's bouquet, I remembered and suppressed a shudder. Thankfully, I'd successfully deleted him from my memory. Monica nudged my foot with hers gently and I recalled that I had to be extra-nice to Twisted Spinster Warden if I wanted a month away from the hostel. 'You're quite right. I don't really fancy flowers, actually. Was it a pretty bunch?' I asked warmly, and gave her my best imitation of a smile.

She waxed eloquent. It was beautiful, apparently, almost as big as a rose bush. I was curious about the sender, but I had to keep her sweet so I patiently heard her out even when she said, 'You must say yes to him, Arti, you really must.'

I nodded compliantly and even broke off a piece of my toast and popped it into her beastly parrot's beak. Twisted Spinster Warden's eyes practically misted over. I knew then that she would be putty in my hands.

The second she left, I tore open the package. There was a shiny horseshoe inside. And a message from Low Life: 'Tried the horseshoe thing. Didn't work. Would rather have you back instead. Call me.'

Charming, absolutely charming. Men just can't handle rejection. Now that I didn't want him any more, I was the most important thing in his life. The insecure, egotistical jerk.

'Honestly,' I told Monica, 'men are assholic. If he really wanted me back, he should have sent me a De Beers solitaire from Zaveri Bazaar instead. I may have considered him in that case.'

Monica raised an eyebrow at me.

'Well, for one second at least,' I hastily assured her and hurled the horseshoe into the bin. My aim was perfect. It sailed right in and hit the bottom with a resounding ring. It was music to my ears, more soul-stirring than Nirvana's *Lithium*. 'I've found god,' I sang in my head.

Monica applauded and said I should send Low Life a parcel with dung in it, accompanied by a message: 'Thinking of you too.'

It was a fabulous idea, but I didn't put it into practice. The idea of shovelling horseshit didn't appeal to me. It wasn't worth the effort, not for a mouldy old ex, at any rate.

Saturday morning, a few days later, saw me outside the hostel with a tote bag, waiting for New Guy to pick me up. Monica rushed out a few seconds later and handed me two raw eggs. 'I think you forgot these,' she said sternly.

'You can't be serious,' I wailed. 'There's no way I'm going to put this on my face, gimme a break Monica!'

'You have to!' she hissed urgently. 'I'm testing out a theory.'

'But I refuse to be your guinea pig! Get a bloody lab rat instead!'

'Just do it for me,' she pleaded.

I refused to take the eggs though and was relieved that New Guy drove up at that very moment. I practically leapt into the car, but Monica, the relentless bitch, followed, and handed the eggs to me through the window. I accepted them silently. I couldn't make a scene in front of him.

'What's that?' New Guy asked conversationally, as we

drove away.

'Oh, just things,' I mumbled vaguely.

'Those things look suspiciously like eggs,' he commented. Damn the bitch, I thought. She hadn't even bothered to conceal them in a packet and I was so flustered, I hadn't noticed.

'Uh-huh,' I said weakly, and looked pointedly out of the window.

'Tell you what,' he said, 'how about we pick up some bacon? We can have a super brekker tomorrow.'

'Great idea! I'll make the chips,' I offered enthusiastically. Whew! I'd got out of that one, I thought with relief. Now Monica couldn't accuse me of chickening out and I literally wouldn't have egg on my face.

New Guy didn't bring up the live-in thing all morning and neither did I. I was quite content with the way things were. But now that Monica had opened my eyes, I was looking for signs that indicated whether we could be compatible as flatmates or not. The mattress, which I hadn't minded before, began to bother me. 'Why don't you get a proper bed instead?' I told him.

'Why do I need a bed? There's nothing wrong with a mattress,' he retorted, looking puzzled.

'It's okay now, but in summer, during the cockroach mating season, they'll be all over us, instead of each other.'

'You telling me you're scared of little roaches?'

'I'm not scared of them. They just give me the creeps.'
They really did. I don't know how many of you know
that cockroaches were imported into the country from
America. They arrived in sacks of rice sent as aid during
a famine, another thing we have to blame the imperialist
bastards for. I'm surprised Calcutta's political parties
don't rant and rave about this.

'Bullshit!' he said. 'You *are* scared of them. Hey, how
can you be, they're so much smaller than humans!'

I knew then that I definitely couldn't move in with
him. Any man who talks like that needs to get his IQ and
testosterone levels tested. 'Oh, for God's sake, don't
give me that smaller-than-humans crap! Size doesn't
matter, despite what men in locker rooms believe.'

New Guy looked at me quizzically. 'Hello there, Arti!
Has this got something to do with the fact that I've asked
you to move in with me?' He's pretty smart.

'No. Yes, yes.'

'So are you saying yes?'

'No, not yet. Not until you get a proper bed.' I had
a very good excuse for exhibiting middle-class values
finally. I'd play for time till then, I decided.

'Done!' he said triumphantly. 'My mum's got an old
divan. I'll move it in here.'

'But that's a single bed!' I said, horrified.

'Hey, a single bed is more romantic,' he argued.

'No way! We'd get cricks in our necks and spondylitis. That's not romantic. I need space,' I gasped.

What do you know? That weekend, I discovered that marriage might not be such an easy thing. The way I looked at it, people who took the plunge were brave souls. But it was an enjoyable weekend nonetheless and I was sorry to be back at the hostel on Sunday evening. Monica and Jo were both out when I got in. Ten minutes after I'd said a lingering farewell to him, I was lying in bed listening to Crosby, Stills & Nash's *Our house* and really missing New Guy. Absence does make the heart grow fonder. He'd given me this book, *Garfield in Love*, really funny and cynical stuff, and I was cracking up over it, laughing out loud, when Monica barged in. 'Did you do the egg thing?' she demanded peremptorily.

'Nope, we ate them instead. Scrambled, with cheese, just the way I like it.' I diverted her attention before she could progress to the predictable 'chicken' invective. 'Ooh, how soppily romantic!' I gushed. 'Dev's given you a heart-shaped box of chocs!'

Monica blushed. I mean, *really* blushed. I was astonished. It wasn't like her to get coy and girlie at all. 'They're not from Dev. A client, actually.'

'A man or a woman?' I demanded.

'Man,' Monica admitted and blushed deeply again.

I sat up, excited. 'All righty! I'm all ears. Spill the beans.'

She shrugged and modestly said, 'Oh, nothing to get orgasmic about. Just an Australian client. I think he fancies me a bit.'

'So go for it, Mo,' I urged. 'If Dev can two-time, so can you. It's only fair.'

'But not with an Australian, for god's sake! I can't deal with whites.' She wrinkled up her nose distastefully.

'Why not? They're also human!' I was about to launch into Shylock's anti-racism speech from *The Merchant of Venice*, you know the one that goes, 'If you prick us, do we not bleed? If you tickle us, do we not laugh? If you poison us, do we not die?' and suchlike, but Monica cut me short.

'The thing with whites,' she said disdainfully, 'is that they use toilet paper instead of soap and water.'

'Ah, no big deal,' I scoffed. 'If you ever marry your Aussie, knock toilet paper off your shopping list and invest in a bidet instead.'

'Oh, shut up! Besides, I love Dev. Despite the fact that he's been acting strange, lately. Very, very strange, sort of not there.' Monica's voice trailed off. She sounded really depressed, but I didn't ask her to expand on it. She'd vent when she was ready, I figured. It would be wrong to push her. To distract her, I told her about another of my nagging problems: was it ethical to bonk your client's brother? She agreed that it wasn't and that I really should get off her account.

fourteen

I went to office the next day determined to make the Creative Director roll up his sleeves for some drastic brand realignments. I prostrated myself before him but he refused. I was informed that all the other writers there had threatened to resign if they were assigned Frankenstein's Monster's brands. 'Unemployment before professional humiliation' was their mantra. He said he'd hired me because he thought I had the balls to say 'Balls!' to her. I wanted to tell him to stuff it, that I didn't give a rat's ass about professional humiliation. All I was worried about was my professional and personal life overlapping. I bit my tongue, however, since it sounded pretty feeble and slunk out of his room muttering politically incorrect epithets under my breath.

I was even more incensed when Frankenstein's Monster called and told me she wanted at least five optional campaigns for her brand to choose from before 5 p.m. that evening. 'Time is running out. The campaign has to be launched before the shelf life of the product expires,' she told me sarcastically.

I sullenly worked them out. My heart wasn't in it and

neither was my mind, which was not a bad thing really, because Frankenstein's Monster evidently wanted soulless, mindless crap. I refused to attend the meeting, although the Creative Director genially offered me a Dutch-courage shot of Scotch. He threw in a stale pack of airline salted peanuts as added incentive. I dryly informed him that I wasn't brought up to accept bribes; my family was never in politics.

With that out of the way, I brooded darkly over my problems and came up with two solutions: a) Quit and get another job; b) Swallow my pride and implore New Guy to marry me before Frankenstein's Monster could do any relationship damage. Since only the first option was doable, I called the headhunter. She flatly refused, saying that she hadn't received her commission for this job yet and warned me to stay put or else. I called another headhunter who pessimistically informed me that the market was down. I'd have to cool my heels for a few months. Damn! I wished I could have confided in New Guy, but I could hardly tell him that I'd rather have Attila the Hun or Ravana as a client than his insufferable, autocratic, brain-dead sis.

I had no choice but to resort to Plan B. I needed expert advice for this, not the usual agony-aunt drivel, so I snuck out in the afternoon on the pretext of bank work, to meet the world-famous-in-Bombay astrologer and asked him whether my relationship with New Guy would terminate in a happy marriage or just terminate. The world-famous-in-Bombay astrologer scrutinized my palm and pronounced that it might or might not work out. There was a fifty-fifty chance. Desperate, I asked him if I would ever get married at all. He peered deeply into my palm again, cleared his throat and said that there was a fifty-fifty chance. I'm sure he's a retired All India Radio weather forecast man. I contemplated telling him that there was a fifty-fifty chance that I would pay him, but coughed up just in case he cast an evil spell on me. After all, he knew my planetary configurations and if he was into tantric stuff, I'd be in deep shit.

When I left him I seriously toyed with the idea of turning into an astrologer myself. I just needed to pick up a second-hand DIY Cheiro palm-reading guide from the pavement, light a few stinky joss sticks and rent a grungy room to get people to pay me respect and mega bucks for looking erudite while sitting on the fence. Incidentally, he still didn't invite me to his haveli to admire Noor Jehan's *farmans*. I was 100 per cent sure I was never ever going to go back to him. I'd have preferred my mum's nutty ex-astrologer who shuddered when he saw my horoscope and pronounced in dark tones that I was a dreaded *maanglik*. The first man I married would die immediately after. I'd have to marry a tree first, and only after lightning or a woodcutter struck it would I be ready to marry a human. I was okay with that. Hey, I was only thirteen when I found out and it sounded pretty thrilling. Almost as special as being told I had a rare blood group. I told Mum about a nice eucalyptus tree I'd seen in Kodaikanal that I'd like to marry, but she was horrified. She tore my horoscope into tiny shreds and said she didn't believe in this foolish astrology crap. I discovered many years later that she'd got a new, fake horoscope drawn up for me with really good stars, the sort that would make prospective in-laws salivate and beg to have me in their family *without* a dowry thrown in. I told you, that woman is a force to reckon with. She even stands up to powerful planets.

Anyway, I returned to office as clueless as I was when I left it. The only thing I knew for certain was that I'd have to come up with a Plan C pronto or else I'd be hitting the cough-syrup bottle like a maniac again. A servicing flunk was lurking around my desk, grinning like the Cheshire cat in *Alice in Wonderland*. He slapped me on the back and said that the 'Lollipop' campaign was almost through.

'Which option?' I asked in a bored way. All of them sucked as far as I was concerned. They were proposition-led. I was not remotely surprised Frankenstein's Monster liked them. They were so dull, even the manufacturing details on the crimp of a toothpaste tube would have made far more gripping reading matter.

'Oh, the headline from one ad, the baseline from

another and the body copy from a third.'

'Fuck her,' I thought to myself. 'If she wants shit, I'll give her shit.'

When New Guy called that evening, I couldn't resist asking him if he was adopted. He cottoned on and laughed. 'Ah come on! You should give her a hard time back.'

'Sugar baby love, as a fellow ad person you're morally bound to give her creative appreciation classes at home.'

'Sure, I'll start with photography on condition that you're the nude model.'

I laughed wickedly and left it at that, thinking that he was taking great interest in my relationship with his sister. If I wasn't a natural-born pessimist, I'd have said that he was seriously considering taking me off the shelf.

I was away in Lonavala for a few days to participate in a dumb, corporate let's-motivate-our-slaves-to-perform-better conference. The idiots! If they'd given us the money they'd spent on the food and acco instead, we'd definitely have been more motivated. It was a total waste of time. All we did was abuse our respective livers.

The next time I met New Guy I was in for a big surprise. A very unpleasant one at that. I was waiting for him outside my office that evening and I almost swallowed my chewing gum when he drove up. I mean, hello, there was this sultry-looking bimbette with big knockers in the front seat next to him——my rightful place. And she had these extra-wide lips, the kind that men associate with great blow jobs. *Calm down. Take a few extra-deep yogic breaths,* I told myself. *She has every right to be there. I mean, why should she take the back seat when he's alone in the front? He's not a chauffeur or something.* I expected her to move out of her seat when I approached. After all, *I* was his babe. But she stubbornly sat there *in my place.*

I have this weird thing about places and people. I don't just adopt them, I'm their slave for life. Even at home in Calcutta, I had my own chair at the dining table and I just couldn't eat a thing if a guest appropriated it by mistake. It was mine, dammit. Mum thinks I have this major insecurity problem. She'd read an article in an American mag and picked up this dumb buzz phrase: 'separation anxiety'. I never heard the end of it, especially after Leeladevi, the Nepalese maid who'd brought me up from the day I was born, left us to take up a more lucrative offer. Mum, of course, still arrogantly maintains that she sacked her because she was worried that I was way too dependent on her. 'Really Arti, you were stuck to her like Velcro. I had to peel you off her for your own good.' She said it like she was doing me this great big favour or something. I still haven't forgiven Mum for it incidentally. I went through total trauma. My kindergarten grades slipped badly that year. I deliberately misspelled 'god' as 'd-o-g'.

I wept for months on end and refused to respond to Leeladevi's replacement. And then, one day in the park, there was Leeladevi playing with a toddler, her new charge. I flung myself into her arms and felt so much at home inhaling her heady tobacco-and-rum-laced breath. She hugged me back with equal ferocity and saying goodbye to her that day nearly broke my heart. It took me years to get over her, longer than it took me to get over Low Life. I guess that's why rum is my favourite tipple. The sickly-sweet smell of molasses reminds me of Leeladevi, bless her wherever she may be.

Anyway, to get back to Silicone Sheena, the woman who wanted more than just my place in the car. The name fitted her like a glove, because she was completely artificial, it was evident that even her breasts weren't made by god. She was introduced to me as New Guy's latest servicing flunk and I discovered that she lived in his neighbourhood and had recently begun to take lifts from him daily. To work and back. I also figured that she had the desperate hots for him. Her voice became at least five levels huskier whenever she addressed him. I had to suppress the urge to offer her cough drops. Also, the hemline of her skirt rode unnaturally high up on her thighs. It just had to be deliberate. I had to quell my insane desire to yank it down. And I was really pissed off at having to take the back seat. I wished New Guy had a car like James Bond. Then I could have pressed an 'Eject' button to catapult her out of my life.

I forced myself to swallow my bile and decided to find out more about her; you know, that know-your-enemy shit you learn at school? She proudly told me she was a Miss India runner-up. New Guy let out a low whistle at that. I deflated her by asking, 'Which number runner-up?' She reluctantly admitted it was eleven. That made me feel really good and I sweetly told her that that didn't really count. I decided to needle her further. 'I bet,' I said cattily, 'when the judges asked you who your role model was, you said Mother Teresa.'

'Hey, how did you know?' She looked genuinely surprised. Boy, was she dumb!

'Oh, all of you say that,' I said superciliously, 'and I can't imagine why. I mean, if she really was your role model, wouldn't you be visiting the slums in your spare time instead of getting bikini waxes done? Why can't you guys be honest and say it's Cindy Crawford or Linda Evangelista or whatever? I mean, can you name even one Miss India who's actually donated her contest earnings to Mother Teresa's outfit?'

New Guy darted an astonished look at me, but I refused to meet his eye. I knew I was being deliberately rude, but I didn't care. Silicone Sheena just shrugged. She ignored me thereafter and concentrated on New Guy instead. She suggested that we go out for a drink.

I caught New Guy's eyes lighting up at the prospect in the rear-view mirror and swiftly nipped her suggestion in the bud. After all, I didn't want to spend the rest of the evening watching her maul him. I firmly said we had lots to catch up on and suggestively ruffled his hair. I even moaned suggestively and throatily when I did that, a fact I'm deeply ashamed of now. I mean, how insecure can one get?

The minute she left, I attacked New Guy. He was hugely amused at my paranoia and reassured me that she had a devoted boyfriend, so I could breathe easy.

'What do you mean breathe easy? The air is so thick with her cloying perfume, I need an oxygen mask.'

'Want mouth-to-mouth resuscitation?' he offered. Clearly, he was still taken with me.

I gratefully accepted, not because I'm an exhibitionist, but because she was still lurking around. I tossed my head back in the classic Scarlett O'Hara-being-kissed-by-Rhett Butler pose and hoped like hell that she'd notice. That ought to have dealt the final blow to her obvious crush on him. But she was made of sterner stuff. Like rats and roaches, she'd survive a nuclear war.

After we got back home, I brought up Silicone Sheena again. I must have had a premonition, because she really bothered me. New Guy wasn't amused any more, however. 'Hell, give me a break, Arti. This possessive shit really puts me off. I love you, that should be enough.'

I broke into The Who's wildly exuberant *You better you bet*. This was the first time that he had uttered the L-word, and it meant a lot to me. After all, every woman with a grain of self-preservation knows that, just like in the alphabet, there's a good chance that the L-word will be followed by the M-word. We spent the rest of the evening billing and cooing to each other like noisy pigeons during the mating season. But I should have paid heed to the veiled threat behind his 'This possessive shit really puts me off' statement. I really should have.

fifteen

The next morning I plotted to leave early so we could leave Silicone Sheena behind. But it wasn't possible, not with one bathroom in the house. That's another thing married people must take care of or they'll get divorced within the first week. Share a bedroom by all means, but not a loo. The slut arrived half an hour before schedule in fire-engine red temptress garb. She looked like she was going to an MTV awards function do or something, not to work. I raced her to the front seat. I had an unfair advantage over her—I had the car keys. I could feel her hostility all through the drive to town. I just couldn't deal with her hovering around New Guy like a starving vulture. It made my blood pressure soar.

I called Monica first thing when I hit the office. She sounded deeply sympathetic and warned me to be on my toes. 'This Silicone Sheena definitely sounds non-biodegradable. She's here to stay. Also, get right back down to earth about the L-word. It still doesn't mean he's going to marry you. And maybe he only said it to shut you up about Silicone Sheena.'

I was sweating like I'd eaten a handful of raw green chillies. 'So how will I know if he's cheating on me?' I whined.

'Easy peasy,' she said. 'If he starts giving you expensive presents, he's doing a number on you.'

'How do you know this?' I persisted.

'Oh, I should know. Dev buys his wife diamonds every other day,' Monica said cynically with a hard note in her voice. 'I even help him choose them. And believe me, I select the flawed ones. I'm an expert. They're supposed to bring bad luck,' she added spitefully.

Wonderful. I had no clue what I should do and tossed between hiring a detective or buying daring G-string panties, despite the fact that they looked like they'd be terribly uncomfortable. Eventually, I did neither.

I wasn't supposed to be meeting New Guy that evening, but I badly needed a drink (or two, or seventeen) after a meeting with his bloody sister. She had deliberated for four and a half hours over whether we should say 'and' or 'but' in a sentence. I returned to office a shadow of my former self and staggered into the Creative Director's room to debrief him on the meeting. He tut-tutted sympathetically and offered me a Scotch. I accepted it gratefully and after I had knocked it back in one giant gulp, he thrust a brand new cellphone in my hand and heartily said it was my new perk. I eyed him suspiciously. Even a greedy, grasping, out-to-get-as-much-as-he-can-out-of-the-company person knows that a cellphone is not a perk, it's a bloody curse. You're officially on call twenty-four hours a day, like a surgeon. And unlike him, not at liberty to loftily pronounce, 'Can't talk now, I'm in a life-saving situation.' I extracted the truth out of him and he reluctantly admitted that it was Frankenstein's Monster's idea. I started hyperventilating and after he handed me a paper bag to breathe deeply into, he patted me on the back and said, 'Relax, she just needs hand-holding till the "Lollipop" campaign breaks.'

'Why don't you just put me on a goddamn leash and get it over and done with?' I suggested bitterly before I strode out.

I was going to fight the system, I decided. If I misused the phone for personal calls, maybe they'd take it back. I surfed the Net for sex-chat numbers to waste time and office money on. After all, once they found out I'd been doing sleazy things on their money, they'd definitely revoke the perk. I'd rather be called a depraved lesbian than be called by Frankenstein's Monster. I was wondering whether I should dial Pendulous Pam or Twin Peaks Patty for a naughty chat when New Guy called. He was very excited about the phone. 'Hey, great, now I can whisper dirty things into your ear late at night, even when we're not together.'

'Whisper them live into my ear tonight, then,' I groaned. 'I'm, like, totally stressed out. Let's go for a drink.'

There was this long, uncomfortable pause. And then he said he had other plans. Usually, I don't question statements like that. But he said it so guiltily, my antennae twitched.

'Oh? What plans?' I said that quite sharply.

He breezily informed me that Silicone Sheena had lost a bet with him and that she owed him a drink. He didn't ask me to join them.

'Ooh, lucky girl!' I said. 'She's lost a bet, but she's won the big bumper prize.' My voice was positively dripping with acid.

New Guy hastily said he had to dash off for a meeting and that he'd call later. Slippery eel, I noted, a whiz in the art of deception. My honeymoon period was obviously officially over. Silicone Sheena was out to get him. And with knockers like hers, I was sure she'd definitely win. For the first time in my life, I wished I'd had the foresight to include Wonderbras in my lingerie collection. I'm quite dumb and guileless, if you really think about it.

My blood pressure was rising even higher while my spirits sagged and on the way back to the hostel, I made an emergency stop at the chemist's. Mr Shah was delighted to see me and asked if I wanted my usual. I nodded glumly. Men may come and men may go, but cough syrup goes on forever. I would, I'd decided, knock back a full bottle and blast a few existential bye-bye-love, bye-bye-happiness numbers on my tinny player. I'd already worked out the medley in my head: the soppy Moody Blues's *Go now*, Pink Floyd's dark *One of my turns*, Emerson, Lake & Palmer's *C'est la vie*, Joan Baez's *Diamonds and rust,* Duran Duran's *Come undone* and Diana Ross's dripping with emotion *Touch me in the morning*. That would do for starters, I thought.

I entered the hostel to discover pandemonium within. Twisted Spinster Warden was howling heartbreakingly into a handkerchief while beating her breast, and ass-licking hostelites were rushing around yelling, 'Polly! Polly!' in a frenzied way. The bloody parrot had flown its gilded cage. God, we'd both been given our walking papers on the same day. I shot into my room and twisted open the cap of the cough-syrup bottle pronto. I couldn't hold out a second longer. Just then, the bloody parrot landed on my shoulder and screeched, 'I love you, Arti, I love you, Arti.' Horrified, I shooed it away, but it perched itself on my chair and continued to tell me that it loved me like a looped phone-answering service. I downed the entire bottle in one big gulp, buried my face in my hands and sobbed for about half an hour till Monica discovered me. I mean, if that wasn't a bad omen signalling the end of my relationship with New Guy, I didn't know what was. It was as dramatic and bizarre as Shakespeare's lions whelping in the streets and spirits rising out of graves to announce the assassination of Julius Caesar. And the worst part was, this wasn't even inspired fiction, it was really happening to me then.

Monica came up to me with deep concern and hugged me till Polly made his/her (still don't know its sex) presence felt. 'I love you, Arti,' it screeched again and Monica shook with laughter. She knew how paranoid I was about parrots. 'Oops, sorry! Am I doing a *coitus interruptus?*' she jibed.

I sobbed louder. 'Get that sodding satanic beast out of my room!'

She obliged. While she was restoring Polly to its rightful lover, I mixed the few remaining drops of the cough syrup with an antacid. I needed extra help that night. The result was a sickly, milky-pink liquid.

'Ugh! What's that?' Monica asked with a shudder when she returned.

'I call it a Life-Sucks cocktail. It's not bad. Try it,' I suggested, and handed my tooth mug to her.

She choked and handed it back. 'Yecch! Honestly, Arti, you should marry your chemist.'

'He won't have me. No man, not even a blind, one-armed leper will,' I said glumly.

'What? Trouble with Aditya?' she asked astutely.

I nodded. 'As I speak, Silicone Sheena has probably

reached third base with him.' I threw Monica out after that. I didn't have the emotional strength to explain. The cough syrup had made me woozy. All I wanted then was music to ease me into my altered circumstances.

I woke up the next day to the shrill ringing of my new cellphone. It was New Guy sounding cheerful. 'Hey, why aren't you in office yet?'

'Omigod, it's past eleven, shit, I'm late.'

'What *were* you up to last night?' he said teasingly.

Then I remembered that it was not what I was up to, it was what *he* was up to that had kept me awake till the crack of dawn. 'What time did you get back home?' I asked abruptly.

'I don't remember. I was too plastered,' he said just as abruptly.

'Oh? Plastered? Interesting. Are there other things about last night that you're too plastered to remember?'

'Cut it out, Arti.' He sounded angry. 'You don't own me.'

'Sure I don't own you, like *you* don't own me. Pardon me for thinking we were in a committed relationship.'

'That doesn't mean we're not allowed to go out with friends,' he said, and sounded decidedly aggro.

'Oh, right! Date-a-friend. That's a game two can play.'

'Look, this is getting too heavy for me. I need a break.'

'Sure, take this lifetime off,' I said coldly. I was okay.

After the previous night's music fest, I was fine. Not 100 per cent cured, but there were encouraging signs that I'd manage to get there. I'd already mentally divorced him anyway. Take my word for it—good music is better than shrinks.

'That suits me fine. Cancel the Goa booking you made for this weekend,' New Guy snapped.

'God!' I said, 'You're really ridiculously practical. I didn't even think about it. And sweetie, I ain't going to cancel it. I can bloody well go with a date-a-friend.'

'Fuck you!'

'Fuck you too,' I said sweetly, but he'd already slammed down the phone. I made my first call on my cellphone. It was to Low Life. 'Hey Sandy, want to meet for dinner tonight?'

sixteen

Of course Low Life, the cretin, did want to meet for dinner. If I'd asked him to accompany me to an arty Lithuanian subtitled flick, he'd have enthusiastically agreed. He was going flat out to please. And I was determined to make it worth his while. I bunked office that day on the pretext of mild flu and fixed an appointment with Shaun, a charming gay hairstylist I'd met at one of my ad shoots. We'd got on like a house on fire mainly because we'd male-bashed with no holds barred. Shaun had looked at my hair with a shudder and offered to make me look presentable. I'd declined then. You know how it is, when you're attached, you're foolishly complacent about appearances. But now that I was practically single, I needed his services badly, on an SOS basis.

'Hmm,' he said, after critically examining my hair, 'do you want to look hot or cool?'

'Remember the iceberg the *Titanic* rammed into? I want to look as formidably frigid as that. I'm dating an ex tonight. I want to fuck his happiness, not his body.'

Shaun sighed deeply. I can swear a tear glistened in his

eye. 'I know what you mean. I just got dumped last week.'

I gasped. 'Not that banker you were madly in lust with?'

'The very same chap,' he groaned. 'He left me for his summer trainee, a bloody woman at that! I can sail through weekdays, but weekends are a nightmare.'

'Hey, what are you doing this weekend? Want to spend it with me in Goa?'

Shaun's countenance visibly brightened. Goa really is magic. 'Why not? It's better than drinking myself silly alone.'

It was settled. My booking wouldn't be wasted.

'I must warn you,' Shaun mumbled, as he went snip snip, 'I'm not into women. I'm not hetero-flexible.'

'And I'm as straight as they come,' I warmly assured him. 'I promise I won't sneak a peek into the bathroom when you take a shower. And we'll insist on two single beds.'

Low Life arrived ahead of the appointed time for dinner. I was gloriously flattered. Hey, at that moment I needed reassurance that I wasn't a total write-off. He took me to this really fancy five-star restaurant where the waiters looked like they were distinguished members of the House of Lords or something and spoke with cultivated Oxbridge stutters. A wine steward hovered over us attentively as I browsed through the list. I'd voted out rum that night. I needed something lighter. Hell, I needed all my wits about me on my first reunion date with my first ex. 'Um, I'll have a Bloody Mary and he'll have a virgin,' I informed the waiter.

The steward nodded solemnly and cross-checked with Low Life.

'A Virgin Mary, sir?'

'No, no,' I cut in impatiently, 'get him a virgin and something to drink too.'

The steward looked puzzled, but Low Life was shaking with mirth. After he composed himself, he told the steward to get him a vodka with fresh lime and bitters and then he squeezed my hand real hard. 'That's what I really miss about you, Arti. You made me laugh.'

'And you made me cry,' I informed him dispassionately and snatched my hand back.

He leaned forward and tucked a lock of my hair behind my ears. I felt like I was being raped. The thing is, I still felt like I technically belonged to New Guy; we hadn't signed the release papers yet.

'*Don't* do that!' I barked.

He jerked his hand back. 'Sorry. It's just that I can't get used to the fact that you're not mine any more.'

'Oh, you put up a great pretence when you were with Bimbo Dogess,' I cut in, with a tinge of undisguised bitterness in my voice.

Low Life winced. 'Look, Arti, I told you that was the

biggest mistake of my life. We all make mistakes.'

'True,' I nodded sympathetically, 'you made yours with Bimbo Dogess. I made mine with you.'

'God, you've really become hard! What happened to your Romeo-and-Juliet eternal love crap?'

'Oh, you were right. That was total crap. I'm over that if-I-can't-have-you-I-don't-want-nobody-baby shit. And we'd kill each other if we got back. Of that I'm certain.'

Low Life grinned. 'Hey, I'd never kill you! I'm into make-love-not-war. And I'm ready to prove it to you right now, in the back seat of my car.' Low Life could be funny in a raunchy sort of way.

'God, you have a one-track mind. Down boy, down! Roll over and play dead.'

He didn't grin. In fact, he became so intense I almost didn't recognize him. He leaned forward and locked eyeballs with me. 'Who's the guy I saw you with? You having a scene with him?'

'Yup,' I blithely lied, but I didn't want Low Life to think I was between relationships. I was pretty vulnerable then and I was sure he'd wear down my resistance. I didn't want to be trapped in a dead end relationship again. Never again.

He pursed his lips. 'How long have you known him?'

'Um, six months?'

Low Life pooh-poohed that scornfully. 'That's bullshit! We went around for four years, Arti. We had history.'

'Did I ever tell you history was my least favourite subject at school?' I shot back.

'Let's give it one more chance, huh, Arti, huh?'

Suddenly, I felt sick. I got this vivid flashback of the closet scene and all the excruciating pain of rejection came back. 'What *did* you see in her?' I tried very hard to keep my voice steady when I said that, but it wavered quite a bit.

Low Life exhaled dramatically. 'Nothing. Mindless sex. Look, it's a guy thing. I was smarter than her. That's what made her so attractive.'

'So, what you're saying is that intelligent women are unattractive, huh?'

Low Life smoothly said, 'Not at all. I wouldn't be begging you to take me back if I thought that.'

'Dream on, Sandy! That woman's been around the block so often, I'm sure you have AIDS by now. I'm not ready to die for the love of you.'

My cellphone rang and I glanced at the caller ID impatiently. I wasn't expecting New Guy, I wasn't that stupid any more. But I was expecting a close relative of his. It *was* her. I ignored it and Frankenstein's Monster rung off. And then she called again and again, the persistent bitch. I had no choice but to answer her call. 'Sorry,' I said, faking breathlessness, 'I was in the shower.'

Frankenstein's Monster sounded pissed off. All she

wanted to tell me at 11 p.m. was that she'd finally decided that the disputed word in the ad copy should be 'and', not 'but'. Bloody electronic leash, I thought angrily, as I switched off the phone. When I looked up, Low Life was giving a babe at the opposite table a salacious once-over. I tilted his head around to face me. 'See? That's what I mean, Sandy. You share Clinton's gene pool.'

'Huh? Hey, hey, looking's allowed. And I swear I'll never leave you for anyone. Except, maybe, Pamela Anderson.'

'Like you'd get that lucky.'

'Exactly,' he grinned. 'That's my way of saying I'll always be faithful to you.'

I decided to give him a test. 'Okay, get real. If you really, really care for me like you say you do, answer this question: if I were your sister, would you allow me to date you?'

He did a mock-shock. 'No way. Absolutely not. That's incest. Hey, I have morals, I'm a good Hindu boy.'

'Oh, you're impossible!'

I quite enjoyed myself at dinner. Low Life was at his ingratiating best. It was like balm for my bruised ego. We were the last to leave. The waiters had practically started stacking chairs on top of each other and they looked at us with barely concealed hostility. We had to leave a really fat tip to mollify them.

On the way back to the hostel, Low Life said he'd pick me up at the same time tomorrow.

'No way, you presumptuous insect!' I protested.

'Ah, come on!'

'I *told* you I'm seeing someone. This was a one-off.'

Low Life gave me an appraising look. He had a glint of steely determination in his eyes and he said very softly, 'I wouldn't bet on it, if I were you.'

'You know what, Sandy? I'd rather have a root canal than go around with you again.'

He lightened up. He looked like he was really confident that he'd win me over again. After all, I used to be crazy about him. 'You've had too much to drink, you don't know what you're saying,' he said indulgently. He leaned over and kissed my cheek as I got out of the car. I spontaneously kissed him back and our lips brushed for a brief second. It felt kind of natural.

As he drove away, I looked ruefully after the car. Obviously I wasn't as immune as I thought I was. I listened to Emerson, Lake & Palmer's *Still...you turn me on* over and over again. And that night, I dreamed about Low Life in the closet again. He had a woman in his arms and when the woman turned her head, I saw her face clearly and woke up screaming. The woman was me. Out of the frying pan and into the fire, those were the plans the Bitch Goddess Fate had in store for me.

seventeen

The next evening I was at Lust Bug's apartment, helping Jo move her things in, now that the marriage was round the corner. My efforts were rewarded with booze and I was hopelessly smashed, the only thing I really have an awesome talent for. It was Day Two of my break-up with New Guy; I had the perfect excuse to drown my sorrows. I'd have drunk anything gladly those days, even nail polish remover; when you're depressed you stop being choosy. I told them about my date with Low Life and they looked at me incredulously.

'You *what*?' Jo said, narrowing her eyes in a menacing sort of way.

'You heard me. I had dinner with Low Life. And I really had a good time. It felt like being home.' I was exaggerating, but I was feeling defiant.

'Have you had a lobotomy or what? Rahul, talk sense into her,' Jo appealed to Lust Bug.

Lust Bug squirmed. He's a really nice guy, but a bit laid-back. 'Um, that's really not my place. But Jyotsna's right, Arti. That wasn't a smart move.'

I raised my eyebrows at him. 'Oh, so the smart move

would have been to cry into my pillow over New Guy's shitty "Let's see other people" plan of action?'

They looked surprised again. 'He said that?' Lust Bug's eyebrows shot up comically.

'Yup. The way this guy's making me sweat, I need truckloads of deo to keep my cool.'

'Hmm . . .' Lust Bug considered, 'he *is* playing games with you.'

I nodded furiously. 'Don't all guys do that? Most follow a four-stage formula. It starts with Bread's *I want to make it with you*, goes on to the Police with *Every breath you take*, then typically shifts gear to U2's *With or without you* and ends with a grand Queen finale: *I want to break free*.'

Jo told me I was just being cynical.

I glared at her. 'Oh, right, this is your cue to tell me there's a man out there somewhere waiting to get my name tattooed on his biceps.'

'Not biceps. Heart,' she corrected me.

I gagged. I mean, that was so banal. 'Heart? Give me a break, Jo! A heart is just a machine that pumps blood. It's as romantic as a water pump.'

Jo didn't give up. In fact, she laid it on real thick. 'Look, Arti. Forget both Low Life and New Guy, by all means. But don't give up on love. There's a Mr Right looking for you as I speak.'

'What's with men? They never get their directions

right. If he's really keen to find me, tell him to go straight to hell. That's where I live, that's my permanent address,' I said bitterly. I staggered to the bar to fix myself another drink.

'Uh-uh, Arti, I think you've had enough for tonight.'

'Correction, Jo,' I said, and raised my refilled glass at her. 'The only thing I've had enough of is men. I want my parrot now.'

Lust Bug looked bemused. 'Parrot?'

Jo grinned and patted him on the thigh. 'It's a long and gruesome story. I'll save it for later, like when we're stranded on a desert island or something.'

I cried that night. Not for Low Life or New Guy, but for myself. I was out there, all alone, again. That really stank. I knew I didn't have any energy left to squeal over baby pictures of other guys again or suffer tedious getting-to-know-each-other moves, forget falling in love.

Goa was therapeutic. I didn't touch a drop of cough syrup and I had carried a six-pack. I was sure that the sight of couples making out on the beach would creep me out and make me long for New Guy or Low Life (I wasn't exactly sure which one any more) in a schmaltzy *Nights in white satin* way, but it didn't. Shaun was vastly entertaining. He told me lots of interesting things like men having the equivalent of premenstrual blues every once in three months or so. 'It's called TDS—Testosterone Depression Syndrome,' he said. 'Maybe, that's what Aditya's going through now. He'll crawl back to you when the mood swing passes. Anyway, you've just had a silly fight. You have to learn to play games.'

'Forget it. The only game I'm interested in playing is Monopoly. And I don't want to discuss men any more. I'm on a break.'

'Okay, but promise me you won't go back to your Low Life. Remember one simple rule in life: go forward, not backwards.'

I nodded and deftly changed the subject.

Shaun had brought some grass along and it went down well as a beer chaser. That's what we did all day on the beach; we lived like lotus-eaters. It was glorious. And when the sun hit us, we were flying higher than kites. This, I discovered, was way more uplifting than shitty love. No guy had ever made me feel this happy. When Shaun confided that he wanted a baby, I even offered him an X chromosome if he required it, I was *that* high. He wept with gratitude and offered me his Julia Roberts wig and feather boa in return. I hope he never remembers the conversation. I'm just not into making babies. It seems like such a brain-dead thing to do.

On our last night, we went to the disco at the hotel and I have to say that in drag Shaun looked way, way hotter than most of the women there, including me natch. We were getting steadily smashed as usual, when the DJ played *What's up,* my favourite militant-chick song by 4 Non Blondes. Shaun and I leapt to the floor in a frenzy and soon we were joined by women, only women. Their boyfriends sat alone at tables looking really pissed off. I overheard one of them muttering darkly to another, 'I hate these male-bashing songs. Now that bitch will refuse to put out tonight.'

The other guy agreed, 'Yeah, and even if she does, she'll behave like she's sleeping with the enemy.' Men don't have any interests apart from sex. I guess that's what makes them so easy to forget. A couple of guys tried to hit on Shaun and me when we got back to the table, but we shooed them away.

'Why, are you lesbians?' one pointedly jeered, hoping to embarrass us.

We both nodded in unison. And I kissed Shaun full on the lips to underline our point. After all, a picture is worth a thousand words. That was a holiday I'll never forget. Who needs diamonds? A gay guy is truly a girl's best friend.

We got back to Bombay with our noses peeling unbecomingly. We both looked like 'Before' ads for venereal disease. Our souls, however, were flawless. I felt happier than I'd felt in ages. I was so over New Guy, I even deleted his number from my cellphone. That's why when he called after about a week, I was unpleasantly surprised. Mainly because I'd started feeling needy again.

The bastard interrupted my healing process, peeled the fresh scab off my wound. I was bleeding profusely once more. He wanted to meet.

'What! Have we both died and been reborn without me noticing?' I icily said. 'We'd fixed a date for our next life, remember?'

'Cut the crap, Arti. We have to talk.'

'What about? Will gay marriages kill family values? Should India have a common civil code? Is euthanasia ethical . . .' I was really warming up, but he cut in.

'Actually, I was thinking more along the lines of "Do neurotically possessive bitches have the right to nuke good relationships?"' he said smoothly.

The world is made up of two kinds of women: those who are appeased by flowers and chocolates; and those who are suckers for words. I caved in. The long and the short of it was that we met for a drink. We behaved like polite strangers till alcohol worked out the reticence. I'd become a wimpy marshmallow again and agreed to lighten up on the date-a-friend deal. After, of course, he agreed to give Silicone Sheena a wide berth. It was a win-win situation.

We went back to his place to kiss and make up and I even smiled widely at Leery Liftman when he gave me his customary once-over. After a much needed make-out session, the temperature dropped considerably. New Guy wanted to know what I'd been up to all those days apart, and we fought like street dogs when I spilled the beans. The worst part is he thought he was morally superior. 'I don't care if Shaun is gay. I just cannot believe that you shared a room with a guy.'

'Fuck you!' I interjected angrily. 'You're the one who said we could date friends.'

'I never said we sleep with them,' he shot back.

'Well, I didn't screw him. Women don't turn him on.'

'Suppose he was bi?'

'Well, he wasn't.'

That shut him up a bit. But then he took off on my dinner with Low Life, that's what he was *really, really* mad about. He was hopping mad, in fact. Mainly my fault, I guess, because in the early days I'd told him how stark raving crackers I was about Low Life. Hey, if I was, I was.

'You don't date an ex, dammit! Everyone knows that an ex leads to sex!' he fumed.

Bitch Goddess Fate intervened during our heated argument. My cellphone rang. It was next to New Guy, and Low Life's name flashed on the caller ID. He grimly handed me the phone. The argument was over. He'd won. Even though I didn't take the call, New Guy was afflicted by a case of emotional leprosy. It was too late to cab it back to the hostel, so we slept in different rooms. Well, I didn't exactly sleep. I lay awake, staring at the ceiling, noting that the fan needed a desperate scrub-down. It was caked in grimy shit—just like my life. I thought I'd paid for my past sins with Low Life, but evidently that wasn't enough. I must have been really evil, a serial adulteress or something in my last life. That's why I had such bad relationship karma. I had no clue what other crap fate had in store for me, but of one thing I was sure: I was going to die alone and undiscovered for days, like Simon & Garfunkel's *Most peculiar man*. I leapt out of bed as soon as there was light and slunk out of the house. Believe it or not, the hostel felt like home sweet home.

eighteen

In *Annie Hall,* Woody Allen says that life is divided into two categories: the horrible and the miserable. I totally agreed with him, then. I felt horrible being single. And utterly miserable in a relationship. I had reached the stage where I really couldn't tell which one was worse. I decided to reread the existentialists again, so I wouldn't give a damn for anyone or anything. Camus's dispassionate opening line in *The Outsider*—'Mother died today. Or maybe yesterday, I don't know'—was the stuff I needed to set me straight. That day, I really wished I were a lesbian. Women are easier to live with than men. They don't give you heartburn or stubble burn, squeeze toothpaste from the middle of the tube or spend entire Sundays surfing sports channels in a dumb-ass way. More important, a relationship with a woman doesn't come with an asterisk that reads 'Conditions apply'. And we can even borrow each other's clothes. The only thing that held me back was the sex part. That's a major obstacle.

I had a lousy day at work, too. Frankenstein's Monster insisted that I include a parrot in the 'Lollipop' launch film for brand memorability. Fate evidently wanted to rub my nose into it. 'Oh god, no! Not a parrot,' I moaned.

'What's wrong with a parrot?' she demanded.

'Um, they're so done to death. If you want a talking bird, let's go with a mynah instead,' I pleaded. I couldn't tell her the real reason. After all, not too many people are aware of the spinster–parrot nexus, so they won't understand my phobia.

The parrot won. Hey, she was footing the bill. And Sigmund-fucking-Freud was probably guffawing and slapping Bitch Goddess Fate on the back.

That evening, Monica and I accompanied Jo on a shopping spree for household crap. We didn't volunteer, we were forced into it at gunpoint. I don't know why Jo insisted. We were so out of it all and agreed with everything she picked up, even garish Karachi-pink toilet seat covers. Both of us were gloomy and distracted. On the cab drive back, Jo was in the window seat and I heard her gasp at a signal. It was like a chain reaction. Involuntarily, both Monica and I glanced out of the window and echoed Jo's gasp: Dev and his obviously-pregnant wife were outside a fertility clinic. And *I* thought I had problems. Remember that goosebumpy quote, the one that goes something like, 'I was crying because I didn't have shoes and then I saw a man who had no feet?' I felt like a total fake. Monica didn't break down initially, though. She looked a bit pale but she was composed, despite the fact that her face became tight and white and she clenched her fingers. Jo and I were silent. And then Monica broke into a brittle smile. 'Well, I'm meeting the shit for dinner tonight. I'll sort it out.'

We nodded, hey, we didn't know what to say, and then Monica's face crumpled. She clutched my arm and asked for my advice. 'Oh, god. I don't know what to say to him, Arti. Help!'

'How? I'm not the relationship expert here. You are.'

'I need your biting sarcasm. Tell me how to bring up the topic without sounding desperate.'

I thought long and hard. Her problem was more important than dog food or lollipops, after all. Then inspiration hit. I launched into my screw-him-into-confessing scheme. 'Okay, here goes. First of all, insist on dinner in an open-air joint. Be warm and friendly. Order the most expensive champagne on the menu and wildly extravagant starters like caviar or truffles. Only after the champagne has arrived do you begin. Point out the brightest star in the sky and say, "Hey, that star is really bright, huh? Do you suppose another child born out of immaculate conception is on its way?" Chances are, he'll say, "Huh?" or "Why are you getting religious on me?"' Monica and Jo were nodding solemnly as I continued. 'Then, you very, very casually say, "You know the Bible predicts a second coming, right?" He'll look puzzled, you're still being macro here. And then you go in for the kill and say, "Today, I saw this pregnant woman whose husband swears he never sleeps with her. Now, is that immaculate conception or is she cheating on him or what?" He'll get it. And then you pick up the champagne bottle, pour the contents over his head and say "Fuck you, Dev. Hope you make a better dad than a husband.'"

Things didn't go according to plan. And the city's pollution wasn't to blame, the stars were shining brightly that night. Monica later confessed that the sarcastic lines worked, but what I had forgotten to script out was her reaction. She didn't have any directions for that, so she completely collapsed after she splashed the Dom Perignon over his head. Jo had gone out with Lust Bug that evening and I had fixed a date with Low Life, hey, I needed an ego massage. We both happened to return at the more or less the same time and Jo accosted me in the lift. 'Was that Low Life I saw you with?' she asked threateningly.

'Nope, his twin,' I slurred. I was flying. Jo began a sanctimonious lecture, but I cut her short. 'Look sweetie, New Guy wasn't exactly an angel either. And if all men are creeps, I'd rather hang out with a known devil. I can't go through all the mind-fucking that new relationships call for any more. I'm old and tired. I even have crow's feet, dammit, I'm scared to smile.'

Jo glared at me. 'Maybe Monica can knock some

sense into you.'

But Monica was in no frame of mind to do anything of the sort. We entered her room to discover that she was higher than I was. Hell, she was swigging whisky straight from the bottle and doing a Tom Petty *Freefalling* sort of dance. I smirked at Jo and told her that, for a change, it was my chance to knock some sense into Monica.

'I'm free,' Monica sang, 'free to fall in love again, free to date and hold hands in public instead of scurrying into dark shadows like a cockroach.'

'Free for what else, your royal highness?' I teased.

She collapsed on the bed with a moan and broke down. After many, many years, the floodgates had opened. And there was a helluva lot of pressurized water in there, waiting to get out. I hugged her and Jo joined me on the bed and suddenly shrieked. She'd sat on a sharp object which turned out to be an empty strip of sedatives. She silently held it up for me to see, but her eyes were flashing an unmistakable SOS.

We swung into action. I did the sticking-fingers-down-the-throat routine, while Jo bribed the watchman to let us out and get a cab. There was no way we could allow this to become public—Monica would be thrown out of the hostel. That night was the longest night in my life, longer than the lousy night I'd thought I was pregnant. Death is more devastating than birth. Jo and I sat in the hospital's waiting room in complete silence. Anything we said would have sounded trite. I really prayed. I was certain my pleas would fall on deaf ears, though. My family wasn't remotely religious. The only temples we'd ever visited were at the ancient temple complex at Khajuraho, not to pray but to gape at the sexually explicit sculptures on the walls, they were way more daring than *Playboy* centre-spreads. Looking at them made me wonder how come us Indians had never managed to beat Russian and Rumanian gymnasts at the Olympics. Mum had insisted I see them as part of my sex education, because I positively refused to read the books she'd thoughtfully bought for me when I hit sixteen—stuff like, *Everything Your Parents Never Told You about Sex* and *Valley of the Dolls*. She was terribly worried I was a prude. Honestly it was a horrible experience, but you'll only know what I mean if you've ever been unfortunate enough to watch a porn flick with your parents. Dad and I squirmed through the tour of the temples, especially when Mum kept badgering the obsequious guide to explain the significance of every pose. I heard Dad hissing to her, 'What do you mean "significance"? It's just perverted sex, dammit! Let's go now.' Anyway, for now I only had my Catholic school assembly prayers to fall back on. Would 'Our Father who art in Heaven' work for someone who wasn't baptized, I mused, as I mumbled the Lord's prayer. I told you, in times of crisis, unimportant, unrelated issues occupy my mind. Maybe it's just an in-built defence mechanism or something.

Lust Bug joined us shortly and Jo fell into his arms and sobbed uncontrollably. Her raw emotion filled me with revulsion. At the same time I realized that she was the best friend Monica and I had. We'd always accused her of being judgemental while she was actually being protective and very, very smart. If Monica had listened to her maybe she wouldn't be where she was. I was suitably chastened.

After many, many hours the doctor emerged from Monica's room. We heaved a sigh of relief when he said she'd survive. He treated us like shit, though. He was shaking with rage. 'You can go in. She's fine. But I want to have a serious chat with all of you before she's discharged. Do you know it could have been a criminal case?'

The three of us rushed into the room. Jo and I hovered around Monica while Lust Bug stood silently in a corner. Monica was looking pale and wan. She squeezed her eyes shut when she saw us. 'No lectures, please. Never knew it would hurt so much. Guess I loved him more than I thought I did.' Her voice sounded far away and weak.

Jo hugged her, but I was ranting. 'Fuck him, Monica. Don't fuck yourself. No man is worth it.'

Surprisingly, Lust Bug supported me. 'Arti's right. You

should have stuffed the sleeping tablets down his bleeding throat instead.' God, he was really mad. I felt affection for him for the first time. Earlier I had just tolerated him because he was Jo's arm candy.

Jo tenderly stroked Monica's hair. 'You feel okay?'

Monica smiled wanly. 'Like a tragedy queen in a B-grade Bollywood movie, without violins screeching mournfully in the background.'

'I hope that means you'll never try it again,' Jo persisted.

'Never again,' Monica promised and attempted a feeble joke. 'It was a lousy high. I'll try Arti's cough syrup next time.'

'Yeah,' I agreed, and cracked a stupid joke in return. 'Chloroform's the best. That's why you find frogs queuing up outside school labs.'

Monica smiled weakly. Her nightmare, thank god, was over.

nineteen

Life went on as usual. Monica had pulled herself together super fast. I think she was so ashamed of her suicide attempt that she'd called on all her hidden reserves of strength to get back on track. What had happened was something the three of us would never forget, but would never discuss again. Seriously we never have, not even when we drink ourselves blind. The subject is taboo.

Monica was job-hunting furiously. She was determined to make a clean sweep of her life. There was this World Bank job going in New York and she was shortlisted for the interview. She spent every spare second she had cramming for it. She wanted it real bad. Jo was occupied with her wedding arrangements, fighting bitter battles with lackadaisical tailors and haggling with florists and caterers. And I was up to my ears in the 'Lollipop' launch, way too busy to brood over New Guy, during the day at least. The nights were painful, but the separation-angst got less with every passing day. I didn't meet Low Life any more despite his frantic calls. I'd started taking Jo's advice seriously. I had new respect for her judgement.

As luck would have it I bumped into Tenaz at a recording studio one evening. I'd tried to duck and hide, but she saw me and came up. This was the first time we met since I'd pinched New Guy from right under her nose, and I was squirming inside. 'Hey,' I said, pretending I was over the moon with joy to see her, 'how you doing?'

'Fine,' she replied, 'how about you? I believe Aditya and you have split?' She flashed her full set of dentures when she said that. No wonder she was happy to see me. I shrugged and Tenaz gave me a searching look. 'Have you met your replacement?' She beamed a smile at me again in accompaniment to her rub-salt-into-the-wound tactics.

I decided to disappoint her. 'Yeah, yeah, I met Sheena. She's really hot! And they *do* look so good together, don't they? Totally made for each other.' I gushed like I was really delighted for him.

That shut her up. Not a very bright babe, Tenaz. All that Parsee inbreeding must have screwed her brains. I could outsmart her. I was glad I'd met her, though. Now that I knew for sure that New Guy and Silicone Sheena were an item, I was certain I'd get over him sooner. Hope only rears its delusional head when you think that an ex is still available and you fool yourself into believing that he's pining for you too. In love, as in life, everything's an illusion, a *mayajaal*. Us Hindus got that right.

Frankenstein's Monster was as annoying as ever. I'd thought my problems were over after she'd approved the campaign for the 'Lollipop' launch, but she drove me batty over its execution too. We'd shot the film with the bloody parrot, a Brazilian rainforest species with bright, multicoloured feathers and a long tail like a feather duster. It was more expensive than a supermodel, it charged $100 a minute. Amazing, and it wasn't even an international beauty pageant queen. All that was left to complete was the edit and Frankenstein's Monster quibbled over that too.

We were ensconced in the editing suite one evening when her cellphone rang. It was her precious brother I gathered, because she gaily told him, 'Hey, Arti's here. Wanna speak to her?' Ruthless and insensitive as ever, she didn't wait to find out if he'd rather jump from the Rajabai clock tower than hear my voice. She handed the phone to me with a bright smile. I think she was trying to suss out our non-relationship.

Far be it from me to let myself down in public. I said a cheery 'Hi'. I didn't wait for him to speak, though. I breathlessly told him I was busy and I'd call back when I was free. I handed the phone back to her. She looked at me queerly and walked out of the room to continue her conversation.

The moment she was out, the director verbally

assaulted me. 'Get her out of here!' he hissed angrily. 'She's butchering the film. I can't put it on my fucking show-reel.'

I shrugged unsympathetically. 'Hey neither can I put it in my portfolio. It won't even get me a bloody increment, forget a new job.'

She returned and we shut up and looked suitably immersed in the edit. About an hour later, after nixing the seventeenth edit, she yawned widely and got up to leave. 'See me to the car, Arti. I'll fill you in on what I'm looking for.'

I followed her obediently. But it wasn't the edit she wanted to discuss. It was her brother. 'Look, I know Aditya and you are having problems and . . .' she held up a restraining hand and second-guessed what I was about to say, 'and I know it's none of my business, but I think you guys should sort it out. He doesn't seem very happy to me and neither do you.'

My mouth opened and shut wordlessly, like a fish. That was the kindest thing she'd ever said to me in her life. I began to wonder if she was human, after all. 'I'm okay,' I said abruptly, when my power of speech returned.

'No, you're not. You look awful.' The glint was back in her eyes.

'Well, maybe that's why he dumped me for someone else,' I shrugged.

'Hello, there's no "someone else". Not yet, so hurry up.'

I just stared at her. She outstared me as usual then drove away. Her last words were, 'Gimme at least ten edits to choose from tomorrow morning.' She was back in business. She's the daughter Mum should have had. She'd have put Mum in her place and Mum would probably have respected her for that. It's dithering whiners like me that Mum walks all over—in hobnailed boots.

When I returned to the edit suite, the director and editor were goofing off, passionately tearing Frankenstein's Monster into bite-sized little pieces. They looked at me for support, but I just couldn't join in their bitching session. Frankenstein's Monster had just shown me a different side. I had to digest that first. 'C'mon guys! All clients are equally awful.' I reasoned. 'She's only paranoid because she has to answer to a board of directors if the launch flops. And they'll give her a tougher time because she's a woman. It's just a job, as long as we get our money why should we complain?'

They looked at me like I was a traitor. I shrugged. But hey, maybe maturity was beginning to set in. And, of course, the fact that I was soft on her brother.

I suffered the next ten edits debating the merits of grovelling at New Guy's feet. It was late, I hadn't eaten a thing all day and my brains had gone AWOL. I guess that's why at 11 p.m. when we'd packed up, I took a cab to New Guy's. I hate my impetuosity. It always trips me up.

The liftman leered even more blatantly than usual. I ignored him as usual. Outside the door I debated whether to ring the bell or use my key, I still had it in my bag. The key won out. I wanted to surprise him and I entered to the soulful strains of jazz. Even though I was a rabid rock freak, I was beginning to appreciate New Guy's taste in music. And what did I see when I stepped in: Silicone Sheena wrapped in New Guy's arms. I involuntarily gasped out loud, like a victim in a horror movie when the coffin lid creaks open and the music rises to a terrifying crescendo.

New Guy swung around. I must say he had great reflexes and presence of mind. He sharply told me not to jump to conclusions. Silicone Sheena was silent and refused to meet my gaze. I could swear she was gloating. 'Goddammit, listen for a change!' New Guy hastily said. 'She had boyfriend problems. I was merely offering her a shoulder to cry on.'

'Right. Evidently I have boyfriend problems too. So excuse me, I gotta go and find myself a sexy piece of ass to dry my tears on too,' I bit out and flung the keys against the wall. A bit of paint chipped from the impact, I noted with satisfaction.

I didn't wait for the liftman to leer at me again. I bolted down the stairs and leapt into a passing cab. Once in I didn't know where to go. The hostel was a no-no. It was depressing enough already, without my added trauma. I didn't feel like a chat with Monica and Jo. I needed to think first, talk later. I got dropped off at the Taj Hotel instead. The cabbie gave me a lewd once-over as I paid him. I guess he, like Leery Liftman, thought I was a high-class slut. I told him to keep the change with as much hauteur as I could muster. I did a mental toss-up between the coffee shop and the loo. The loo won on account of an ample supply of tissue paper and no chance of being propositioned by randy tourists or sexually repressed locals with migraine-suffering wives. I got a call on the mobile from New Guy, but didn't take it. I switched the phone off instead.

I forced myself to cry, but nothing happened. That made me panic. I feared that I'd overdone the existential brainwash and become like the dry-eyed woman in the tragic poem that opened with something like: 'Home they brought her warrior dead, she nor screamed nor uttered cry.' Hell, I was sure I'd need expensive therapy to cure my emotional paralysis. Then I got this fab, revenge-seeking idea: I called Low Life. I knew that he'd willingly offer more interesting parts of his body than just a shoulder for me to dampen. After all, you have to fight fire with fire. And any fool knows that sleeping with an ex is not as sleazy as a casual one-night stand. It's just a small aberration that helps a dumped woman get centred faster than transcendental meditation.

I called him before I left. If I'd walked in on him necking too that night, I'd probably have killed myself. And on the drive there, I was struck by something funny: I'd always thought New Guy was my transition man for Low Life but now it seemed that it was the other way round.

twenty

Life really is full of unpleasant surprises. But the next biggest one that night was when I discovered that Low Life wasn't the placebo I was looking for. I started weeping copiously when he attempted to French-kiss my pain away.

'Stop it Sandy, we need to talk.'

'We can do both at the same time,' he said reasonably, but I shoved him off. It just wasn't happening for me with him, not any more. I knew I'd need hypnosis to fall in love or even lust with him again.

Sandy was patient with me at first. 'Look, if it's that marriage crap that's making you hold back, relax. This time round I intend to marry you. Really.'

'You said that the last time too,' I accused him.

'Yeah, but I really mean it now.'

Maybe he did, who knows? I just didn't wait long enough to find out. Low Life got really pissed off watching me play a neurotically confused tragedy queen. He stalked into the bedroom and switched the TV on. I heard anguished moaning, I'm willing to bet a bottle of cough syrup that he was watching porn. Anyway, I just sat there in the living room, wishing I could die. You know, of all the sonnets Shakespeare's written, the most moving one, as far as I'm concerned, is sonnet no. 34, addressed to a lover who had treated him badly. And the lines that played in my head that night were: 'Though thou repent, yet I still have the loss/ Th' offender's sorrow lends but weak relief/ To him that bears the strong offence's cross.' Okay, so at the end of the sonnet Shakespeare caves in and forgives his offender for being mean to him, but I couldn't. I can't. I can't forgive. I'm not big enough. That's one of my weaknesses and I really don't think even a psychiatrist can cure me of that.

When the sun rose, I picked up my things and, on the way to the front door, I passed by the bedroom. Low Life was asleep and he looked so vulnerable it made my heart ache. For that one moment, I forgot all the crap he'd put me through. I knew for sure that I didn't love him any more, but that I'd remember him forever. He may have been a creep, but he was a very special one. Our good times had been exceptionally good. I couldn't resist brushing my lips against his cheek. He stirred and opened his eyes sleepily. I whispered goodbye and he sat up like a jack-in-the-box and looked at me pointedly. 'You're not coming back, are you?'

I shook my head.

'So you're saying that I'll finally have to invest in a dictionary to find out the meaning of big words?' he said wryly.

I nodded and turned to leave. I couldn't speak. I had this huge lump in my throat. I knew this really was our final goodbye.

'Wait, Arti.' He leapt out of bed and followed me to the door. We hugged real tight and then I heard this muffled, 'Promise me you won't invite me to your wedding?'

My reply was equally muffled: 'Promise me you won't invite me to yours?'

We both looked at each other with deep understanding. And then I left without looking back. I'm glad he shut the front door after I was out of earshot. It would have killed me to hear the lock clicking in.

When I returned to the hostel, Twisted Spinster Warden was grimly seated at her spy-box. My god, she was there even at the crack of dawn. Being a spinster is no joke, you have nothing to do. She started her usual nonsense about cancelling my night-out passes. I nodded numbly. I was too emotionally drained to put her in her place.

I started throwing things into a big suitcase. I'd decided to go back to Calcutta and sort myself out for a bit, maybe even get a job there. Bombay hadn't been kind to me. Monica and Jo bunked office to organize my life. Their eyeballs shot out of their sockets when I tossed my jars of anti-wrinkle and anti-cellulite cream into the bin. Who needed them? No one was going to look at me anyway, was my rationale. And they were even more astonished when I told them that Low Life had popped the question.

'And you turned him down?' Jo squawked. '*You* said *no*?'

'I said no,' I nodded wryly. God, she still thought I was a pushover for him. 'For one, I'm sure he'd have let me down again. Just don't trust him any more. For two, the thing is, I don't want shits in my life again. Why should I be grateful just because a shit asks me to marry him? I'm not *that* desperate. Even a parrot is preferable to a shit, Twisted Spinster Warden got that right. And you know what? Being single isn't all that bad a deal. Hell, I've finally realized that I'm more miserable when I'm in a relationship than when I'm single.'

Monica did a heartfelt 'Hear, hear!' to that.

I continued my soliloquy with a deep sigh. 'All this love-at-first-sight is bullshit. I wish there could be marriage-at-first-sight. Then we wouldn't have to go through all this painful love crap.'

'You know what, Arti? You're finally seeing eye to eye with your mum. I think you're mentally ready for an arranged marriage,' Monica observed shrewdly.

Jo agreed.

I was shell-shocked. 'Oh god, no! I've hit middle age. That's when daughters become like their mums!' I dove into the bin to retrieve my anti-aging potions and mentally swore to use them daily. The idea of anyone mistaking Mum and me for sisters was way too much to take.

I'd wanted to send the Creative Director a crisis-in-native-village telegram, but Monica insisted I call instead. He was completely hysterical. 'Are you out of your mind? The "Lollipop" launch conference is tomorrow. You can go after that.'

'You don't understand. I have to leave today. It's a family crisis.' Well, it wasn't one yet, but it certainly would be, I thought, when Mum discovered that I'd been dumped yet again.

'Arti, I forbid you to go on leave.'

'Okay, then I quit.' I said that very, very firmly.

'You can't quit!'

'And you can't stop me from going on leave.'

I won.

Then I kissed Monica and Jo goodbye and left. 'You'd better be back in time for my wedding,' Jo wagged a finger at me warningly.

'Of course, I will. Possibly even before that if my Mum drives me crazy.'

Just as I was about to board the aircraft, New Guy called. I let the phone ring for a bit and then answered it. I didn't speak. I just wanted to hear his voice. And then I switched it off. There was a hollow feeling in the pit of my tum and I decided to fill it up with alcohol instead of that crappy airline fare. I'd kept a quarter-bottle of vodka in my cabin baggage in case of emergency and proceeded to knock it back surreptitiously with Coke. Even though I was totally depressed I clearly had my wits about me, because I picked up the puke bag from the seat pocket and kept it on my lap. Alcohol doesn't go down well with air pockets. I started weeping silently, but copiously. The white nosy parker passenger next to me wanted to know what I was upset about. I told her those weren't tears, just a deadly-contagious conjunctivitis discharge. She promptly got her seat changed. Saddam had it right: biological warfare is a far more effective deterrent than nuclear shit. Westerners just can't handle it. Basically, they're wishy-washy wimps.

twenty-one

What I did on that holiday was to completely regress into childhood. I reread most of my favourite authors except Richmal Crompton, Tom Sharpe, Douglas Adams and P.G. Wodehouse, because they were New Guy's favourites too, I didn't want to be reminded of him in any way. Hey, I regressed so desperately I even read Enid Blyton's Brer Rabbit series again. I used to be a diehard fan in my salad days. He was real cool and I'd crack up every time he outwitted Brer Bear and Brer Fox. His nephews, Binkle and Flip, weren't all that hot, even though I'd named my two rabbits after them. And Lewis Carroll had me grinning as broadly as his Cheshire cat again. I'm not too crazy about *Alice in Wonderland*, but I loved *Through the Looking Glass*. I thought it was brilliantly funny. You know what's strange? I have Mum to thank for Lewis Carroll. She's an ardent fan too, and when I was little she'd tuck me into bed and read out the best bits: Alice's encounter with Humpty-Dumpty and her bizarre meal with the Red Queen. We must have gone through those chapters over a million times but each time they made us both laugh out loud with tears streaming down our cheeks. Mum had seen the pantomime in London, but she swears that while it was enjoyable, the book is far, far better. Sometimes I wonder that if Mum had been less controlling perhaps we could have been good friends.

But the passage I reread every night like it was the Gayatri mantra or something was from D.H. Lawrence's *Lady Chatterley's Lover*, the 'It's no good trying to get rid of your own aloneness, you've got to stick to it all your life' bit. It kept me going, it really kept me sane, and more important, it kind of drained the neediness out of me.

I met some of my old school and college pals, all of whom were unhappily married apart from Keya, my radical leftist chum, who was happily divorced. Honestly, she had this glow on her face I'd never seen before. She was *that* happy to be single again. Mum sniffed contemptuously when she found out. She'd never liked Keya. She thought she was a bad influence on me. 'I expected that of her,' she said cattily. 'Any girl who spends her college days burning buses can never make a good wife.'

Mum always made Keya blacker than she was. She'd never burnt a bus; all she'd been guilty of was lying spreadeagled on the road to block traffic when bus fares went up by ten paise. Not for herself, she'd never seen the inside of a bus—her dad owned, like, a stable of

Mercs—but for the peasants, as she insisted on calling them. I thought that was an extremely well-intentioned gesture on her part.

Keya worked as a reporter with a really heavy-duty newspaper and gave me a couple of freelance assignments for their Sunday supplements. Airy lifestyle stuff, like the changing face of club nights (DJs replacing live bands) and suchlike. I was real turned on seeing my byline in print and extremely chuffed when Keya's editor offered me a few more assignments. According to Keya, he was deeply impressed with my style and expressed a desire to have me on board, full-time. I toyed with the idea of switching to journalism and sticking on in Calcutta. After all Jo was leaving the hostel to get married and Monica was leaving too. She'd finally got the World Bank job in New York she was gunning for. She'd called with the news. I'd have no friends left in Bombay, no one to keep me centred when life gave me a hard time. I had nothing to go back for, really. I promised Keya I'd think about it. Privately, though, I'd practically accepted the job. I loved writing stuff that no brain-dead client shat upon. And I enjoyed being in Calcutta. It was as cosy and familiar as being back in the womb. People in coffee houses and bars still had heated arguments over whether Netaji Subhas Chandra Bose was dead or alive, mini buses still swerved drunkenly through the streets screeching to abrupt halts at non-designated stops to

pick up stray passengers and everything was more or
less the same. The only difference was that, with the
communal Bharatiya Janata Party gaining a foothold in
this communist stronghold, the city that had marched to
the beat of left, left, left was now going left, right, left.
That was the only thing that pissed me off. I hate
communal types. Indians are meant to be secular. That's
our real strength. That's why I love being an Indian.
Racism, in my opinion, is a white failing. But apart from
that I was at peace. Only consider: I had taken five
bottles of cough syrup with me and in fifteen days I'd
only finished four. That was a sure sign that the city
agreed with me. And Mum seemed to have changed for
the better too. She asked no awkward questions and let
me be. I was really surprised. I thought she'd be plotting
and planning my wedding with a toothless widower or
a wife-beating divorcé now that I was almost thirty, way
past the age of making a good match.

I was lulled into a false sense of security and confided
in Dad that I may not be going back. He looked pleased
and said I was always welcome at home. He'd really
missed me. But when he broke the news to Mum, all
hell broke loose. She totally lost it. 'What do you mean
you're giving up your job in Bombay? You're earning
lots.'

'Yeah, but I won't be living off you if I stay here. Keya's
paper has offered me a job and I'm going to take it.'

'How much?' Mum demanded, her crass North Indian blood surfacing.

That put me in a tight spot. They were offering me less than half of what I was currently earning. Pay scales in journalism were pretty abysmal. But I would be staying at home so food and acco were free. I could manage very easily, I thought.

Mum wasn't impressed. She snorted and sailed out of the room to plot and plan something evil, I assumed.

I was right. A couple of days later, on a Sunday afternoon, I was lounging on the sofa, reading, when Dad came up to me nervously. He cleared his throat. 'Erm, beta, we have to have a chat.'

'Sure. What about?'

Dad chickened out. I really love him lots, but he's not much support. He's the hopelessly henpecked sort. All he's allowed to take decisions on are whether we should have Nizam's tandoori chicken rolls for Sunday lunch or Zeeshan's mutton biryani. And he's at his grandest, macho best when he measures out the beer for Mum's shandy. He anxiously yelled for Mum to join us. I had a premonition of disaster. Mum strode in, all guns blazing. I could almost hear the theme music of *The Good, the Bad and the Ugly* playing. 'There's this chap coming to see you this evening. Your dad and I are going out. Get into something decent,' she barked without pausing for breath.

Like hell I would, I thought. I ignored her and went back to my book.

'Stop being insolent, Arti.'

'And stop being interfering, Ma. Look, if you don't want me living with you, I'll move in with Keya. She got a two-bedroom flat as alimony. She'd be willing to have me.'

'You'll do nothing of the sort!' Mum thundered.

Dad treacherously took her side. 'Listen, beta, I promise you this is the last man you'll ever have to meet. Just do this one last time. I'll never allow her to put you through this again. You see, I met him this morning and quite liked him. I think you'll like him too.'

'No way, Dad! I'm not into this marriage thing.'

'Just this once,' he pleaded.

I said a firm 'no' and continued to read my book.

At about 5 p.m., they left the house, Mum zapping me with death glares and Dad looking beseechingly at me. 'Fine,' Mum said, 'don't change your clothes. He'll say no to you and then you'll know what it feels like to be rejected.'

As if she didn't know that I already knew what that felt like. I knew so much about it, I could write a goddamn book on it as fat as the bloody *Encyclopaedia Britannica*.

She attacked Dad then. 'Why do you allow her to

pinch your old shirts? She looks so blowsy and frumpy in them. And,' she added, targetting me again, 'you should be grateful that we're leaving you alone with him for a chat.'

I scoffed. 'More fool you! What if he's a serial rapist or something? I'm sure he never mentioned *that* in the matrimonial ad.'

Dad practically shoved Mum out of the house and slammed the door before a full-fledged fight could break out. I heaved a sigh of relief after they left and went back to my book.

About half an hour later the doorbell rang. *Must be the matrimonial asshole*, I thought. I raced the cook to the door. I had to get there first. My plan of action was simple: I'd open the door a crack and tell him that his prospective bride had measles, that the entire house was declared a contagious zone. That would drive him away instantly.

It wasn't him though, just someone peddling bullshit. 'Sorry,' I snapped and attempted to slam the door shut. 'We don't buy that crap any more.'

But New Guy pushed the door open. He was stronger than me.

twenty-two

I'd been set up. Jo had conspired with Mum to upset my life and plans all over again. *Et tu, Jo, and damn you*, I thought, totally pissed off. 'Well, well, what do you know,' I sneered at New Guy. 'A rabid commitment phobe playing earnest matrimonial prospect. How do you sleep at night?'

'Not very well actually,' he said with a cheeky grin, 'I'd sleep better if I were with you.'

'Okay, cut the crap and get out. The door's over there.'

'Not leaving without you. Hey, take your time,' he said generously and sat down, making himself very comfortable. He even started flipping through Dad's book on World War II spies that was lying on the table.

Two could play the game, I thought. I flung myself on the sofa again and resumed my reading. I couldn't focus on a single word, though. My mind was churning furiously.

New Guy conversationally said, 'So you want to get married in Cal or Bombay or what?'

'Don't intend to get married to you,' I bit out.

New Guy went, 'Tut-tut. For shame, Arti. The liftman will leer. And,' he added in a mock whisper, 'people will talk.'

I ignored him.

The cook arrived beaming, with a tray laden with snacks. Mum had obviously briefed her that he was a son-in-law prospect. She looked a bit surprised at seeing us both reading, but she must have thought that that's what educated people did at arranged set-ups. New Guy thanked her nicely, then asked her if she could buy him a pack of fags. I was seething. How dared he order my servants around like he owned them? But I kept silent. I didn't want to encourage conversation.

After she docilely shut the door behind her, New Guy shed his cool and got into aggressive mode. 'Right,' he said, and menacingly came up to me, 'you owe me a bloody apology for behaving like a neurotic, half-witted jerk.'

'How fucking dare you, you lying, cheating shit! I catch you necking with your precious Silicone Sheena and you want me to apologize? What for? For sneaking up on you?'

'I was *not* necking with her! I was consoling her. Her boyfriend had just dumped her for Miss India runner-up no.3, I think ... or was it 2?' He wrinkled his brow.

'Whoa,' I sat up, interested, despite my anger. 'He moved up the ladder—Silicone Sheena was no.13 or something, right?' I have this fascination for the ridiculous. I just cannot resist it.

New Guy chuckled. 'I knew you'd enjoy that. And now that you're finally looking more animated than the furniture, I'm going to kiss you into being more compliant.'

'Oh no, buddy! No way am I going to mingle fluids with someone who believes in that date-a-friend crap and plays dumb, commitmentphobic games,' I bit out and picked up my book again.

He sat down next to me and he talked. Really talked like never before. Yes, he was commitmentphobic, he admitted. The thought of marriage had filled him with extreme revulsion. I was getting under his skin and it made him panic. He had to keep some distance between us. He knew Silicone Sheena had the hots for him. He'd flirted with her out of self-preservation. The necking was completely innocent, though. He'd never touched her otherwise or wanted to. He was sorry. He missed me. He'd lately discovered that he preferred marriage (if that's what I insisted on) to a life without me. That was the gist of his monologue.

I gave him Rhett Butler's classic, 'Frankly, my dear, I don't give a damn' line. He said I was lying. I categorically told him I was not.

'The thing is, Arti, I love you.'

'Hornswoggle,' I spat out.

'What did you just say?' He looked completely at sea.

'I said "hornswoggle".'

'What the hell does that mean?'

'It's Georgette Heyer for unadulterated bullshit.'

'Who the fuck is Georgette Heyer?'

'Visit Google.'

'Sure. After I finish what I came here for.'

He inched closer and I gave in way too easily. It must have been the legendary 'Axe effect'. Damn potent aftershaves. He was evidently intent on breaking the current Guinness Book of World Records kiss, but I foiled his plans. I surfaced after a bit, gasping for breath. I was clearly too out of shape for that and he made me promise to go in for cardiovascular training sessions. He eyed me critically. 'And you desperately need sex too. You've put on weight. Must be all the *mishti doi* you get here. You should be glad I came back. Should we start now?'

'Yeah, sure! If my mum and dad catch us in the act, rest assured we'll have a shotgun wedding.'

'Not a bad idea. The next time you decide to leave me,' he said warningly, 'you'll need my lawyer's consent.'

'Hey, wait a minute! I haven't said yes yet. I have a few conditions.'

'Name them,' he offered.

'Okay. No babies, no joint bank accounts, no inextricable knots. Because if it doesn't work out, I want an easy exit. The door always has to be open.'

New Guy was completely unfazed. That's what I really love about him. He's the ultimate in cool. 'Will do. But you know, Arti, you're exhibiting classic signs of commitmentphobia yourself.'

'Oh, I had great teachers, the best.'

He laughed, then asked me when I'd like to follow him around the fire.

'Actually, I still haven't said yes. I have two final tests for you. One: will you promise to die only after I do?'

New Guy hugged me tight. 'Yup,' he said seriously, 'I promise. In fact, to make absolutely sure that that happens, I'll kill you the minute your menopause begins and you start borrowing my razor for your chin.'

God, I loved this guy with a passion!

'Okay, now for the last test,' I pronounced grandly.

He rolled his eyes impatiently and I vanished into the kitchen and briskly whipped up an egg. New Guy followed me there. 'What? You want to know if I can make an omelette?'

'Nope. I want to know if you can kiss me with this stuff on my face,' I said, and smeared the egg on liberally. I almost threw up, it was *that* stinky.

New Guy was less queasy. He gamely kissed me and said, 'If I'd known you were so kinky, I'd have asked you to marry me a long time ago.'

Suddenly we heard a shriek. The cook had returned

with the fags and caught us in the act. God knows what she thought. Probably that educated people have very strange mating rituals. She's always eyed me strangely since. And I can't ask her for eggs with a straight face any more.

We had a heated argument after that. I wanted to pack my bags and run before my parents got back, but New Guy insisted that we tell them our plans first. I put my foot down firmly. 'No way! I'm going to make her sweat.'

'Don't be childish.'

'Look, I'm not telling her anything till the wedding cards are printed and in the mail.'

'But why?'

'Because if she knows in advance, she'll probably insist that we get married at the Taj.'

'So what's wrong with that?' he persisted.

'The bloody monument, not the hotel,' I explained dryly.

He looked completely baffled. The thing is, he'd never met Mum, only Dad. He didn't know how manipulative and control-freakish she could be. But finally he relented. He had no choice, I was adamant. I left a note for them with the cook, saying that the matrimonial prospect had turned out to be a disaster and that I had decided to go back to Bombay to avoid any more of their arranged-marriage shit.

On the flight back, I was struck with inspiration for the

wedding card. I hastily scribbled it down on a paper napkin and showed it to New Guy. 'You recognize this?' I asked, as I shoved it under his nose, 'it's the line from the Chivas Regal broken-bottle ad. This is the first time in my life I've pinched a line from an international award-winning campaign. Super-Bitch Boss would approve, right?'

New Guy read the headline aloud. It said: 'Have you ever seen a grown man cry?' He squeezed my hand hard, very hard, and said, 'I heartily approve too. You'll make a very understanding wife for a commitment phobe.'

twenty-three

Well, I married New Guy. He's my official 24×7 cockroach-slayer now. I'm still married to him. It's been quite a few years, we've even made it past the proverbial seven-year itch. The door's still open, but we're both inside, despite a few very, very close calls. That's the astonishing part. Marriage isn't easy, especially not in the early days, when you start feeling claustrophobic, like you're stepping into Noah's Ark or something and condemned to live in depressing coupledom. And it ruthlessly strips you of dignity: singles see their loved ones dressed up; couples see their loved ones dressed down, and it isn't a pretty sight. And who pops extra-strong mints to disguise Goan Fish Curry breath any more? Or whispers sweet nothings when there are more vitally important things to discuss, like broken flush handles? God, we've suffered.

And we've aged too. Earlier, when testosterone-heavy guy stuff like *Born to be wild* and *Highway to the danger zone* played on the car stereo, New Guy would zip along at 120 kmph, he just couldn't stop himself. Now, he never goes over a stately, dignified 70 kmph. I call him

Old Guy now. We're steadily inching closer to high-
fibre, low-cholesterol diets. And we've signed up at a
gym for weight-loss sessions—we squandered most of
our sex coupons in our premarital days I guess.

What makes me really happy is that we're not those
pathetic couples you see at restaurants, staring at other
diners because they have nothing to say to each other.
We're smarter. We carry books and crossword puzzles
along. And when some of our friends who are
contemplating marriage come to us for advice, we give
it to them in one word: 'Don't.' Not because we're
unhappy with each other, hey we're as perfect a combo
as fish 'n' chips, but because being single and together
was a lot more fun. But, despite the lack of excitement
marriage has its moments too. Love becomes mellow
and matures into deep affection and understanding. If
you've ever heard Tull's *Wond'ring aloud*, you'll know
what I mean. Look at it this way: most people are willing
to offer you a shoulder to cry on, but not too many
people would still love you if you puke on it instead.
That's the joy of marriage. I have to confess that I'm not
complacent yet. Hey, shit happens. You always have to be
prepared for it. My collection of music-to-get-over-
cretins and existential literature is still there. I've decided
I want them with me on my funeral pyre, just in case
there's action upstairs too. Or in case New Guy and I
split before that, hell, I'll always be insecure.

Although Monica, Jo and I live in different cities, we manage to meet at least once a year. New Guy calls it the witches' convention. He always refers to us as the three witches from *Macbeth* and rightly so, because our farewell words to each other are to the tune of, 'When shall we three meet again/ In thunder, lightning or in rain?'

Jo is based in *Duh*li. Poor thing had to move to the capital after Lust Bug became the political editor of a news magazine. And even worse, she has quintuplets, thanks to in-vitro fertilization. She bitterly complains that her children's birthday parties can be a very expensive affair. Monica's married to a white in New York. But she's got a bidet, so she's got nothing to grouse about. She bumped into Low Life at Frankfurt airport last year. He's posted in Singapore these days and he's in the midst of a bitter divorce battle with his wife. Monica was dying to ask him if there was a second one waiting in the wings, but she held her tongue. He's completely bald now but according to Monica it makes him look sort of dishy. Baldness has finally given him character. He begged her for info on me and she swears his eyes softened when she spilled the beans. I have to admit that my eyes softened too, when I heard about him. I feel this vague sort of affection for him. Which is why, perhaps, I still have a book he'd given me as a birthday present. It was called *King Rat* and he'd written

'To my queen' on the fly page. I've never bothered to read that book, but I can't bring myself to throw it away. It's the only link to him I have left. It's not as precious as diamonds, but it still means something.

And surprise, surprise, after Jo and Monica, Frankenstein's Monster is my best friend. I *told* you life is downright strange. We still don't agree on advertising, but since I have nothing to do with the crazy ad world anymore, I'm not impassioned enough to fight that hard. But I do feel sorry for the ad agency guys she works with, the poor sods. And New Guy's mum isn't a bad sort after all. I mean, she's tough, but well-meaning underneath all that brusqueness. Guess she's been through a lot of shit with an acrimonious divorce and all that. That's one thing New Guy made me promise: even if our marriage collapses, we'll work on our friendship and keep it forever. And, of course, try not to flaunt our new human acquisitions under each other's noses. I promised to try, but I'm not sure I'll be able to pull it off. Why do guys *always* want to be friends with people they dump? I just don't get that about them. They're really weird.

The only person who hasn't changed a whit is my mum. She's still badgering me. Her new trip in life is to become a grandmother, but I refuse to oblige. To shut her up, I've told her that I'm clinically infertile, but she e-mails me adoption centre details every hour on the hour. Guess that explains why I'm still a cough-syrup junkie. Oh, and those anti-wrinkle and anti-cellulite creams? They don't work. Don't waste your money on them, the mirror never lies. I'm saving up for a Botox job now. Check out Demi Moore. She looks like hot shit, even more stunning than her daughters. And hey, this is for all you singles out there: if a commitment phobe is giving you a really hard time, leave him. There's a good chance he'll come running back. Remember what I said earlier? Men only want you when you don't want them any more. I'm willing to place my right hand on a bottle of cough syrup in a court of law and swear that it's true.